THIS BOOK BELONGS TO:
....
....

PRAISE FOR THE CHRISTMAS CARROLLS

'A Christmas book about kindness and cheer to make even Scrooge's heart melt.'
Dame Jacqueline Wilson

'Fizzing with energy and festive cheer, The Christmas Carrolls is a heart-warming must-read for the Christmas period. Mel's writing sparkles like the star on top of a Christmas Tree.'
Jennifer Bell, author of *The Uncommoners*

'Gloriously festive, brilliantly funny and utterly endearing. I loved it.'
Abi Elphinstone, author of *Sky Song*

'As warm and cosy as drinking hot chocolate in your favourite Christmas jumper. A festive feast of fun.'
Maz Evans, author of *Who Let The Gods Out?*

'This book will fill your hearts and souls with joy, sparkle and most of all ho - ho - hope!'
Laura Ellen Anderson, author of *Rainbow Grey* and the bestselling Amelia Fang series

THE CHRISTMAS CARROLLS

For
Emma
X

First published in Great Britain 2021 by Farshore
An imprint of HarperCollins*Publishers*
1 London Bridge Street, London SE1 9GF

farshore.co.uk

HarperCollins*Publishers*
1st Floor, Watermarque Building, Ringsend Road
Dublin 4, Ireland

Text copyright © Mel Taylor-Bessent 2021
Illustration copyright © Selom Sunu 2021
The moral rights of the author and illustrator have been asserted.

ISBN 978 0 7555 0362 9
Printed and bound in the UK using 100% renewable electricity at CPI Group (UK) Ltd
1

A CIP catalogue record for this title is available from the British Library.

MIX
Paper from
responsible sources
FSC
www.fsc.org **FSC™ C007454**

This book is produced from independently certified FSC™ paper
to ensure responsible forest management.

For more information visit: www.harpercollins.co.uk/green

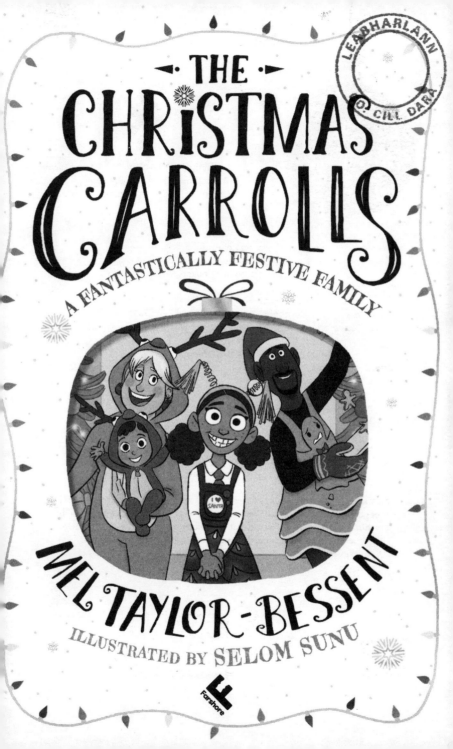

· THE ·
CHRISTMAS
CARROLLS

A FANTASTICALLY FESTIVE FAMILY

MEL TAYLOR-BESSENT

ILLUSTRATED BY SELOM SUNU

Farshore

HOLLY
CARROLL
←

ARCHER

IVY
CARROLL
←

THE BIG IDEA 1

Have you ever had an idea hit you so hard, you nearly fell off the toilet? Let me tell you, friends, it's *quite* a spectacular moment (especially if you slip inside the bowl and make a massive splash like you're on a water ride at a theme park).

"Snow drops and pine trees!" I squealed, pulling myself back out of the toilet. "Of course!"

I dried myself on the reindeer hand towel and flushed the chain. Dad had just upgraded the musical toilet seat, so when I put it down it sang me a gurgling, underwater version of *We Wish You A*

Merry Christmas. I hummed along, counting down the days 'til Christmas as I washed my hands under the candy-cane taps. Dad still hadn't found a way to make them pour red and green water, but he did one time freeze every pipe in the house when he tried to make snow taps instead. Now *that* was a cold winter.

"Hols?" Dad's deep voice called from downstairs. "You ready?"

I hurtled out of the bathroom, grabbed some loo roll from the back of the cupboard, and spread myself starfish-style across the landing floor.

"Coming!" I squealed a few minutes later. I sprinted into the kitchen with toilet paper draped over my head, felt tip scribbles across my cheeks and a bauble-sized lump on my head after crashing headfirst into the banister.

"I'm OK!" I yelled, holding my arms out for balance. "I meant to do that."

Dad looked up from his mixing bowl. His dark cheeks were covered in icing sugar and he was wearing one of

Mum's famous gingerbread aprons. The frills and bells sat in all the wrong places, but I've always loved the way the deep orange colour made his eyes sparkle.

"Snowflake?" Dad beamed, the bell on the end of his Santa hat jingling. "What's going on?"

I cleared my throat and laid the toilet paper on the counter with a flourish.

"I give you . . . *Tushy Tinsel*," I exclaimed. "Why wipe with plain, boring toilet paper when you can experience Tushy Tinsel, the latest invention from Holly Carroll? It's sparkly, festive and fun, it brightens up any bathroom *and* it's extra tough because of the tinsel around the edges."

"Holly!" Dad gasped, his eyes widening. "This is christmariffic. It's festabulous! It's . . ."

"Worthy of going on the Invention Wall?" I grinned.

Dad inspected the toilet paper a little closer. "Absnow-lutely! I assume you've tested it to check that it works?"

I swallowed nervously.

"Hols?"

"Of course," I said, swiping the blotchy paper from his hands and hiding it behind my back.

"Good. You remember what happened the last time you tried to be a clever claus and skip the testing phase?"

I cringed. I had *technically* tested the Tushy Tinsel, but there was no way I could tell him that the red and green ink had smudged and now my bum looked like a baboon with a bad infection.

"Merry Monday!" Mum's shrill voice rang from the hallway. "What Christmas cheer will we spread today?"

She glided into the room carrying my baby sister, Ivy. They were wearing matching reindeer onesies and Ivy was snoring softly on her shoulder.

"Hols is just about to add her latest idea to the Invention Wall," Dad said, smearing a blob of butter across his brow. "Tushy Tinsel. Genius!"

I wrote it in my biggest, swirliest handwriting underneath last week's addition, the *Decoradder*, and stepped back to admire my handiwork. My list wasn't half as long as Dad's (his included the Christmacam – a Christmassy camera –, the Tinsel Tangler and the Unwrapping Gloves,

to name a few), but one of these days I was going to invent something so merrynifiscent, Father Christmas himself would name me the best gift-giver, invention-maker and cheer-spreader in the world. Maybe he'd give me a medal, or at least a personal inventing booth in his workshop?

"Hols?" Dad said, flicking through his *Big Book of Christmas Recipes*. "Can you check the snow-o-meter for me? Something tells me we might just be in for a fluttering of flakes."

"Didn't you say that yesterday?" I laughed, searching the fridge for an early-morning snack.

Mum grinned. "And the day before that, and the day before that."

Dad's brown eyes glazed over as he stared into the distance. "Did I ever tell you about the first time I saw snow?" he said. "When your grandparents moved us from Jamaica to the UK, and the plane landed in a snowstorm? We'd never seen anything like it! We walked straight off the plane, onto the runway and ..."

"Had a snowball fight?" Mum and I said, finishing his sentence.

Dad nodded coyly, still lost in his daydream. "It was nothing short of magical," he breathed, spinning around and scattering half of his Snowflakes and milk across the floor.

As Mum rushed to grab the Chrismamop (Christmas tree mop), I pushed myself further into the fridge and found a bag of chocolate coins hidden behind the brussels sprouts and stinky spinach. I glanced over my shoulder to check they weren't watching – but just as I reached for the coins, my foot slid on the counter (that I was absolutely *not* climbing on) and I tumbled to the ground, bringing half the contents of the fridge with me. To be honest, I would've styled it out had it not been for the giant turkey leg that fell in slow motion from the top shelf and nearly took my head off.

"Hollypops?" Mum said, totally unaware of my near-death experience. "Have you done your morning chores?"

I shot her my most innocent *of course I have* smile, shoved everything back in the fridge (minus the chocolate coins, which happened to fall into my pyjama pocket) and ran into the hallway.

Our morning chores were always the same. Mum checked the light displays and made the beds, Dad cooked up a festive treat in the kitchen, Ivy – well, she was just learning how to walk, but I'm sure she'll have Christmas Carroll chores in no time – and I was in charge of the entrance decorations, which meant checking everything from the snow-o-meter outside to the fake snow sprinkled around the staircase spindles.

Now, I don't know if it's because I developed superhuman speed or because I wanted to hide somewhere and scoff my chocolate coins in peace, but I rehung the tinsel on the tree, straightened the snowman doormat, opened today's door on the Christmas calendar and dusted the giant ice lanterns before Mum finished her first Christmas carol of the day. Next, I checked the lights on the miniature

Christmas village that covered half of the floor, pulled the red velvet curtain open that hung across the door, and stepped outside to check the snow-o-meter.

The snow-o-meter (as if you didn't already know!) is a special thermometer that measures the likelihood of snowfall. Dad taught me how to read it when I was three years old. "The bigger the snowflake, the deeper the snowfall," he'd say, and sometimes we'd even bust out our special snow dance to encourage the skies to open.

With an optimistic spring in my step, I leapt over our Christmas Carroll doormat, opened the door and skipped outside.

Oh.

There wasn't a single cloud in the sky. No chill in the air. Not a single snowflake on the snow-o-meter. My shoulders slumped.

I suppose it was July, after all.

After pleading with the snow-o-meter for a good five minutes (surely my powers of persuasion would work one of these days?) I walked back into the hallway, popped a chocolate coin in my mouth and poked my head around the corner of the kitchen.

There, the sun streamed in from the window and mixed with the clouds of icing sugar that hung in the air. It turned the room into a real-life snow globe, and looked so magical it was like Mum, Dad and Ivy were trapped in a different world.

A world filled with snowfall and sunshine, flashing fairy lights, and constant jingling bells. It was a world where every day felt like Christmas.

Just then, Dad grabbed Mum and twirled her around the kitchen in time to the festadio (festive radio). They laughed and sang, and bust out the sort of moves that made them look like drunk, lopsided penguins.

"Let's spread cheer wherever we go," Mum sang.

"Let's spread cheer with a ho, ho, ho!" Dad added.

Ivy woke from her sleep and added her tiny "oh, oh, oh" two seconds too late.

I smiled to myself. It was another perfect morning in the Christmas Carroll household . . .

     or

         so

             I thought.

CODE 9627

We were having a pretty normal week before the events that changed my life forever. In Maths, Mum taught me about symmetry using lights and decorations on a tree. In English, I wrote a letter to the Royal family to convince them to make 25th June (Half Christmas) an official holiday. And in Art, we designed a fireproof hat for Santa, some hoof warmers for his reindeer, and a new wrapping paper that was so bright I reckon the elves could use it as a tracking device. It was the same week that Dad made giant elf sculptures out of ice to help him forget about the heatwave, and the same week that Ivy catapulted herself from her highchair in an attempt to fly like a reindeer. In my down time, I made a new Christmas cushion, practiced my high C for *O Holy Night* and gave some serious thought to changing my name. I was thinking of something along the lines of Santarina or Christmarella (or something really exotic like Gladys). It was all inspired by Mum, you see. She legally changed her name when she was at university and now everyone just calls her –

"Snoooooow!"

Mum ran out of her bedroom wearing an enormous Christmas pudding hat.

"Code 9627. Code 9627!" Dad shouted. His voice was getting more and more highpitched.

" Code 9627?" I squealed, sliding on to the landing in my light-up Santa slippers. "Really? What is it? What's happening?"

"Are they finally making Christmas last an entire week?" Mum said. "Did the Prime Minister get my letter?"

"Better!" Dad cried, barely able to contain his excitement.

"Is Santa looking for new elves?" I suggested. "Can we apply?"

"Even better!"

"Are we getting snowfall in summer?"

"Are they announcing a new reindeer?"

"Have enough people signed my petition to plant Christmas trees in every garden in the world?"

"Better, guys! Much, much better!"

My mind was in overdrive. Code 9627 was only used in the most exciting, life-changing circumstances. Mum and Dad had only used it twice before – when Ivy and I were born. Was that what Dad was trying to tell us? Were they having another baby? How come Mum didn't know about it? Were they going to call it 'Tinsel' or 'Mistletoe', or my personal favourite, 'Nutcracker'?

Dad stepped forward and took Mum's hands. "It's Sleigh Ride Avenue," he whispered. "Number twelve. It's up for sale."

The colour in Mum's face drained. Her eyes grew as big as baubles and her mouth fell open. Then, with a tiny squeak, she fell into Dad's arms.

She came to with the help of a hot chocolate, two miniature gingerbread men and a rousing rendition of *The Twelve Days of Christmas* by me and Dad. I even added in a freestyle rap to mix it up a bit. "Yo, yo, yo, ma name is Holly. Some people think I'm a bit of a wal—" I'll, er, tell you the rest later.

Sleigh Ride Avenue? Was Dad sure? I thought that was a place they made up in their heads. A dream road in a dream town in a dream life that didn't actually exist. But there was Dad saying that an actual house on Sleigh Ride Avenue had come up for sale, and that ... hang on, what *was* he saying?

Within minutes, the kitchen table was covered in files and paperwork, Dad was on the phone wearing his 'Head Elf' jumper, and Mum was stocking the car up with boxes of mince pies. I kept asking them what was going on, but they were in such a tizzy,

I couldn't get their attention. Instead, I stood on the table, wearing one sock, my tinsel-lined Hollyhood (which was my very first invention), and a Christmas tablecloth as a superhero cape.

Mum always says I should *fill every moment with cheer*. So whenever I'm not coming up with inventions with Dad, studying with Mum, or spreading cheer to other people, I do what I do best: fashionise. Yes, fashionise. I bet you think I'm really clever for coming up with my own word, don't you? You should try it some time. I might even add it to the dictionary. It'll say something like: *Fashionise: to make high-end fashion from everyday items. Word created by invention-maker and expert cheer-spreader, Holly Carroll.*

My best fashionised item of all time was undubidedly (one of my top five made-up words!) the Hollyhood. When I was six years old, I cut a velvet hood off one of Dad's least-worn Santa costumes and attached it to one of Mum's stripy scarves. Then I spent weeks sewing twenty five pockets to it and finding little treasures to hide inside. You could think of it like a fancy wearable advent calendar, but instead of opening a door to find a chocolate, you reach inside a pocket and find some Christmas pudding, your favourite toy, or all the secrets of the universe!* After admiring my latest fashionising efforts, I watched Mum whizz in and out of the house, communicating with Dad via manic hand gestures and eye movements.

"Yes, that's Carroll. Nick Carroll," I heard Dad say. "And don't you worry, kind sir. We will be buying the house today." He stuck a thirty-point plan to the fridge door and scribbled notes on the back of his hand. "We've no need to view it, my good friend. Do you know how long we've waited for a house to become available on this road?"

I jumped down from the table and ducked and rolled around the room like a ninja spy. Dad was so engrossed in his phone call, he didn't notice me swipe a christmallow (Christmas marshmallow) from the plate on the side and pop it into my

*That last one may or may not be true.

mouth. The gooey, creamy, sludginess slid across my teeth and stuck to my tongue. It tasted of lemon and maple syrup and nutmeg and cream and . . . sorry, I'm getting distracted.

I tiptoed to a huge file that Dad had placed on the counter. *Dream Homes* was written on the side and there was a small newspaper clipping on top. The title said: **The Ten Most Christmassy Road Names In The World** and there at number three was **Sleigh Ride Avenue, England**.

Sleigh Ride Avenue is a small road in a quiet suburb of London. With houses dotted at even distances and plenty of land around each one, property on this street is highly sought after, and with one of the most festive street names in the world (second only to North Pole Way in the Arctic and Christmas Street in the United States of America), these homeowners rarely move from the street. Only two houses have come up for sale in the last fifty years.

Dad smiled triumphantly into the phone and gave me a thumbs-up. "My wife is setting off shortly. She has mince pies for everyone and she'll sign the contract as soon as she arrives."

Wait, wait, wait. We were actually buying the house? We were going to live on Sleigh Ride Avenue? Us? The Carrolls? That dream home on one of the most Christmassy streets in the world was going to belong to *our* family? Fireworks erupted in my head. My heart exploded with joy. My scalp started to itch from the melting candy cane I'd lost somewhere inside my Hollyhood.

"Holly!" Dad called. "Grab the christmacam, will you? This is a Christmas Carroll highlight if ever I saw one."

I was one step ahead of him. I grabbed the christmacam from the shelf in the hallway and took a quick elfie before turning the camera on Dad.

"This is one of the best days of my life!" he beamed. He coughed and turned his attention back

・ Code 9627 ・

to his phone, his voice dropping a few decibels. "No, thank you, young man. I'll stay on the phone until my wife arrives. It's only a two- or three-hour drive, and I've got lots of questions to ask in the meantime." He placed his laptop on top of the *Dream Homes* file and strode out of the room.

I glanced at the laptop and saw an email with a few bullet points and an empty box with the words 'photo coming soon' written inside.

Number 12 Sleigh Ride Avenue:

- A five-bedroom home with unique features
- Comes with a mature garden, double garage and off-street parking
- Viewings recommended

An image of a road lined with bushy fir trees and snow-tipped chimneys came into my mind. I imagined every house having immaculate gardens, billions of fairy lights and driveways made from glazed gingerbread. We were going to spread so much cheer. We were going to be surrounded by people who loved Christmas as much as us. We were going to become the most Christmassy community the world had ever seen.

I took a deep breath. Was this really happening? I'd dreamt of moving house forever. Of moving somewhere with actual neighbours and other houses down the street and waking up to different Christmas decorations besides our own. Don't get me wrong, I love our house with the fields and sheep and cows surrounding us, but to get real neighbours with real names that we can wish a Merry Day to will be better than . . . than gravy on chocolate cake!

As I span around the table in glee, Mum hurtled through the front door and whizzed into the kitchen, accidentally knocking me sideways. Then, with all the grace of an overweight yeti on ice-skates, I stumbled into the Christmas tree in the corner and sent a shiny silver bauble crashing to the floor.

"You OK?" Mum said, grabbing her keys and map of *Santa's Shortcuts*. "This is going to change everything for us, Snowdrop. *Everything*. I hope you're ready?"

My heart did a weird fluttery flip thing, like it had turned inside out and back again.

Isn't moving house the same as packing up Christmas decorations? I can box my life up, unpack it at the other end and everything will stay exactly the same, right?

I knelt down and picked the silver bauble off the floor. It had a crack right down the middle.

Oh. I suppose one or two things could get broken along the way?

SLEIGH RIDE AVENUE

3

I blinked and moving day arrived. A man with a bushy moustache and tubby tummy was talking to Mum, his eyes slightly crossed like he was concentrating really hard.

"Now, those photo frames, Trevor," Mum was saying. "They're made from authentic Inari-Saariselka wood and they were shipped from Lapland just for us. You will be careful with them, won't you?"

Trevor nodded and scribbled a note on his clipboard.

"And those kuksas in that box over there . . . they're cups gifted to us by the leader of the Sami people in the Arctic. It's the kind of cup Santa himself would drink from, so please don't break them."

Trevor pointed to the box and a group of people from the removal company scurried over.

"Oh, and mind those pots of cloudberry jam – I made them fresh this morning," Mum said. "And the sleds in the shed have great sentimental value. And the girls' hobby trees are one-of-a-kind."

Poor Trevor looked like he might pass out. I don't know if it was the heat or the size of the job or the pressure of handling such precious goods, but I made a mental note to make him something nice during the car journey. He looked like he could do with a funny poem, or a bobble hat for his bald head, or maybe a sick bag judging by the colour of his cheeks. Aha! Santa sick bags – that was something I hadn't made before! Santa-ick bags? Sickta bags? Sanickags? We'll work on the name later . . .

As we drove away from the house, I shoved my head out of the window and blew it a billion kisses. I couldn't believe we were actually leaving. Memories flashed inside my head like a film projector. All the snow ball fights, the late-night carol singing, the light shows Dad put on just for us. We were really leaving it all behind.

I wiped a tear from my eye and pulled two knitting needles out of my socks to calm my nerves. I brandished them in front of me like swords and then got to work on a moustache-warmer for Trevor, letting the *click-clack* of the needles relax my muscles and lull me into a daydream about the christmassiest Christmas house you've ever seen on Sleigh Ride Avenue.

It didn't take as long as I expected to arrive at the new house, not with Dad's twenty-five stopwatches and perfectly planned schedules. In fact, after scoffing turkey sandwiches, singing along to our Christmas travel playlist and designing a new type of stocking that could double as a santa sick bag, we arrived at Sleigh Ride Avenue before Mum had time to finish her Christmas poems for the removal people.

Dad had barely turned the engine off before I

opened the door and jumped out. I'd been practising my New Home Dance for days and couldn't wait any longer to come face to face with our new house. I started with a twirl and then a leap, and then opened my mouth to sing my special welcome song when . . .

I stopped.

This *had* to be a mistake. A few tall trees surrounded the house, but it had a bland wooden door, dusty brown bricks, and dull grey moss creeping across the roof. Sure, the garden was big enough for an ice rink or two, but the grass was singed and the bushes were bare. It looked like it had been totally forgotten about.

It was lifeless. Loveless. And so Christmasless, it hurt.

I turned around to look at the other houses in the street.

This was . . .

I bit my lip and narrowed my eyes.

This was . . .

My heart pumped faster inside my chest.

This was . . .

Not at all what I expected.

Where were the reindeer on the roofs? The wreaths on the doors? The million fairy lights to outshine the stars in the sky? Surely this wasn't the place?

It took me a moment to let everything sink in. The houses that lined the street didn't display a single candle, bunch of mistletoe or strand of tinsel. In fact, some of the houses were so dull and grey, it looked like no one lived in them at all. This *couldn't* be Sleigh Ride Avenue, the third most Christmassy road in the world. Could it?

As Mum, Dad and Ivy ran down the path and

disappeared through the front door, I closed my eyes. *It's just a hallucitation,* I told myself, praying the road would be filled with snowfall and inflatable singing Santas when I reopened my eyes. *It's just the excitement playing tricks on me.*

"You there!" a voice snapped behind me. "What's going on?"

I whirled around to find a man so hunched over, we were practically standing nose to nose.

"Oh!" I jumped, backing away from his leathery face and the cluster of sharp grey hairs that sprouted out of his nostrils. "Merry Christmas! My name's Holly Carroll. Of the Christmas Carrolls. Are you having a joyous day?"

The man looked at my outstretched hand with sasspicion (when someone looks suspicious but in a really sassy way).

"*A joyous day?*" he snarled.

"Yes. Have you been spreading cheer? Have you sung your morning carol yet? Would you like to see my New Home Dance?"

"New home?" He waved his giant nose from left to right as he looked at the row of moving vans. "This is *your* new home?"

I nodded, wondering if I should speak a little louder. "WE. ARE. THE. CARROLLS. AND. WE. HAVE. JUST. MOVED. TO. SLEIGH. RIDE. AVENUE. DID. YOU. KNOW. IT'S. THE –"

"Please stop," the man said, waving his hand at me like I was a fly hovering over his Christmas dinner. "Exactly how much longer will these trucks be blocking up the road?"

"Oh, not long," I said, forcing my smile a little wider. "We just need to offload forty-five Christmas trees, the contents of Dad's workshop, Mum's old apron collection, two hundred and ten festive cushions, ninety boxes of tinsel, the monthly wreaths and memory wall photos, the –"

The man raised his hand. "I hope you're not expecting a welcome party," he spat. "Here on Sleigh

Ride Avenue, we don't tolerate parties of any kind. We keep ourselves to ourselves and that's the way we like it, do you hear? We don't block up the road with enormous lorries. We don't play loud music. We don't leave our rubbish bins out any longer than is required. We don't rev our car engines. Children don't play in the street. And singing is frowned upon."

I threw my head back and laughed uncontrollably. "Singing is frowned upon!" I howled. "That's a good one, Mr . . .?"

"Blug," the man said, turning his back to me so he could glare at the removal men and women. "Hume Blug."

"Your name's HUMBUG?" I gasped.

"No, no, no," the man groaned, pulling a face like I'd forgotten to flush his toilet. "My name is Hugh Berg and I am the longest standing resident of Sleigh Ride Avenue. In fact, I . . ."

"Hols!" Mum's voice shrilled from inside the

house. "Come on, Snowdrop. It's mince-pie time!"

My stomach grumbled right on cue.

"It was a pleasure to meet you, Mr Bleurgh," I said, grabbing his hand and shaking it as hard as I could. "Congratulations on being the longest stale rodent of Sleigh Ride Avenue. What an achievement! What house number do you live at? I'll be sure to bring you some mince pies when they're ready. I could even bust out my inflatable elf costume, if you like?"

"Mince pies?" the old man mouthed. "Elf costume? In Ju—"

"Merry Monday, Who Bleurgh!" I shouted, leaving him standing on the pavement surrounded by removal people carrying giant boxes and towering Christmas trees. "Have a cheeringly good day!"

THE ANNOUNCE-MENT

4

W hile Dad started building his workshop in the garden and Mum scrambled into the moving van to dig out our elf costumes, I explored the rest of the house. First I found an oven big enough for roasting the fattest of turkeys, then a blank wall in the hallway to list our inventions, and a cupboard that was just about wide enough for all of our snow shoes, but then I found something so shocking, something so despicabelly horrendous, something so mindboggingly unbelievable, I thought I had tripped into an actual nightmare.

"MUM!" I bellowed. "DAD! Code 96 . . ." Wait.

What was the code for the worst news ever? Did we have one? *Why* didn't we have one? "Code I-need-you-here-NOW! Now, now, now, now, now, now, now."

Mum sprinted into the living room wearing half an elf costume, and Dad poked his head through the window.

"What's all the shouting about?" Dad said. "Ivy's napping."

I couldn't bring myself to say it.

"Look around," I said, my voice shaking. "What's missing?"

Mum and Dad looked at the ceiling and into the corners of the room.

"What?" Mum said. "What's wrong?"

"There's no . . . no . . . no . . ."

Mum stepped closer and wrapped her arm over my shoulder.

"There's no . . . no . . ." I burst into tears. "There's no *fireplace*."

Ivy lifted her head from the cot in the corner and started crying. Mum's face turned paler than Santa's beard. Dad practically fell through the open window.

"NO FIREPLACE?" Mum gasped.

"How will we sing carols around a fire?" I wailed. "Where will we hang our stockings? How will Santa visit us without a chimney?"

Mum crumpled to the floor and buried her head in her hands.

"Now, now," Dad said, nearly breaking his leg as he climbed through the window. "We can have a fireplace installed. The best fireplace you've ever seen. The biggest, the smartest, the Christmassiest fireplace in the world. How about that?"

But I was already shriekobing (that peculiar noise you make when you're not sure whether you want to shriek or sob). Dad tried to calm me down with breathing exercises and the promise of pre-bedtime carols, but this was a Christmas emergency like no other. I mean, how would *you* react if you discovered an essential part of your house – like a fridge, a toilet, a front door, or indeed, a fireplace – *didn't exist*? I bet you wouldn't sleep for weeks either.

"Maybe it's time to tell Holly the news?" Dad said, his eye twitching as he glanced at the fireplace-less wall.

News? What news?

"Please don't tell me there's not enough electricity for our Christmas Eve light display either? I don't think my nerves can take it," I gulped.

"We have something for you," Dad continued. "We've been thinking about it for a while and we think it's finally time. Snow, do you want to do the honours?"

Mum forced a weak smile as Dad helped her off the floor. "Now that we're living here, we're going to have to make some changes, Snowdrop," she said shakily.

"Your mother and I have discussed it," Dad said. "And we think it's best that we both get full-time jobs so that we can afford all of the improvements we have to make on the house."

"I'm going to re-open Snow Carroll Apron Designs and your father has been offered work at the garden centre," Mum said. The corners of her mouth twinged and she played with her hands nervously.

"Riiiiight?" I said. "Is that it?"

Mum shook her head. "We want to show you this," she said, reaching into her apron pocket and handing me a booklet with a shiny red cover.

"It's a school prospectus," Dad explained. "For the local primary school. Now that we need to work during the day, I'm afraid we won't have time to homeschool you as well."

I stared at the sopectus. The spaplectus. The spla . . . whatever it was called. Children in the picture were smiling up at a tall, slim woman, who I could only assume was a head teacher. Hesitantly, I flicked through the pages. They were filled with information on the different classes and teachers, but I got that same nervous feeling in my belly that I had when I found out we were moving.

"Do they have Christmas plays?" I said quietly.

Mum nodded. "They do."

"Do they have Christmas carol concerts?"

"Two," Dad said. "One for parents and one for the local village fair."

"A nativity?"

"Of course."

"And . . ." I gulped. My entire response balanced on this next answer. "What colour is their uniform?"

Mum and Dad smiled at each other. "Red," they said together.

For a moment, my body froze. School. An actual school. Me – Holly Carroll – was going to school? I jumped off the rug and punched the air.

"Are you serious?" I shouted. "This is amazing! It's winterful. It's bauble-illiant. It's a Christmas miracle!"

"There's only one slight hiccup," Dad said, kneeling in front of me so I could see every little laughter line. "School starts in a week. We'll have to sort your uniform, your school supplies and everything else in the next seven days. Are you OK with that, Snowflake?"

I couldn't believe what I was hearing. I was going to get the chance to spread cheer, not just to the postman or the lady at the supermarket or other neighbours along the street, but to whole classes of children, and maybe some teachers too? This was what I'd always wanted. It was what I'd been working towards. It was what I knew I was destined to do.

"And there's one more surprise," Dad said, reaching inside a giant sack that he'd hidden behind the sofa. "I made you this . . ."

As he brought his arms forward, I gasped. "Dad!" I squealed. "What *is* that?"

He beamed. "I call it the Backpack of Cheer."

The backpack was in the shape of Father Christmas's head, and it was so huge, Ivy could fit inside it. Twice. There was even a giant pocket inside the beard for my pens and pencils. I took it from Dad with shaking hands and eyes as wide as snow globes.

"Ho, ho, ho!" Dad's voice bellowed out as soon as I touched the strap. "Merry Christmas!"

"Dad!" I cried. "It's your voice? In a bag?"

"Only took me eight attempts to get it right," he said, holding his belly and beaming proudly. "What do you think?"

I ran forward and flung my arms around him. "This is the best!" I grinned.

"Now you'll be with me wherever I go."

As Dad spun me around in the room, Mum let out an exaggerated cry and buried her face in her apron. I don't know if it was the emotion of sending me off to school, the shock of not having a fireplace, or my excited fart that slipped out a few moments ago, but she looked like she could seriously use a santa sick bag.

"Well, Hols," Dad said, placing my feet back on the floor and striding across the room to comfort Mum. "Do you think you're up for it?"

I stared at the school booklet thingy. "Yes!" I smiled, all thoughts of the missing fireplace and unbearable heatwave fleeing my mind. "Get me to school!"

SPREADING CHEER WITH A HO HO HO 5

The last week of the summer holidays was so scorchting hot, it was almost impossible to go outside. But true to his word, Dad arranged for someone to install a fully working fireplace within a few days, and we kept the fire burning the entire time, letting the warm flames and oaky smell bring the house to life. We spent the rest of the week painting each brick red and green, and hanging our stockings on big gold hooks along the top. I even added logs and piles of kindling to huge buckets sitting at the side, and made some new reindeer cushions for the sofas. With Mum's ceiling of fairy lights and fake snow on the windows, not to mention a new festive door bell and Christmas-shaped pebbles on the path outside, I found myself enjoying the house a little more every day.

Over the weekend, Dad baked his famous grotto cakes, we sang bedtime carols on the lawn (I'm sure the neighbours appreciated this even if they didn't come out to tell us), and I made plans to make Lockerton Primary the first ever school to run on cheer!

I admit, I hadn't been sure about all the changes to begin with. The new house, the new town, the new school . . . But then I realised, what if all my learning over the last nine years had been for this? What if I was supposed to pass on my knowledge and experience in spreading cheer so that children become more cheerful, and then they turn into cheerful adults and then we have a more cheerful world? I mean, don't give me a Nobel prize or anything, it's not rocket science, but – actually, I've got space on my trophy shelf if you're offering.

By Monday morning I felt prepared and ready for anything. I had a twenty-five point plan with ideas for how to spread cheer at school, a stack of first-day Christmas cards, Mum had sewn pom-poms on to the front of my elfsolls for PE, I had enough tinsel in my hair to outshine the sun, Dad promised we could have a house-warming party with all the neighbours, and my Backpack of Cheer was going to be the talk of the town!

"You ready, Snowflake?" Dad yelled from the car, tooting the *Jingle Bells* horn and giving me a thumbs-up.

I took a deep breath and grinned. "As ready as a reindeer on Christmas Eve," I said.

❄

I walked into the Lockerton Primary School office expecting a welcome from a kind-hearted, round-faced lady with glasses perched on the end of her nose and wrinkles as deep as Santa's sack, but that, apparently, is not how they make school receptionists any more. Oh no. This lady had a short, blunt bob, a pointy nose and squinty eyes that said, *I'm watching you and don't you forget it!*

"Name?" she barked.

"Carroll," Dad said, giving her his toothiest grin. "First name, Holly. She joins Year Five today."

"Form?"

Dad fumbled in his back pocket and pulled out a single sheet of paper that he'd covered in ribbon and stars.

"Dickens Class," the woman said, eyeing the piece of paper sasspiciously before shoving it in a tray. "Across the playground. Second block on your right."

"Dickens?" I squealed.

"Dickens?" Dad repeated.

"Dickens?" we yelled together.

The receptionist tutted loudly. "That's what I said."

"As in Charles Dickens? The man who wrote *A Christmas Carol*?"

The woman's squint hardened, like she was

thinking incredibly hard or trying to blow Dad's head up with her mind. "Is there any other?"

My heart was doing that strange skip-a-beat thing again. How was this all happening? Moving to Sleigh Ride Avenue. Going to school for the very first time. Being placed in Dickens Class. How many more of my Christmas dreams would come true this week?

Dad spun me around the school office and out of the door. He screamed out "Weeeeeeeeee!" like he did when I was five years old and I flung my head back and laughed. A few kids jumped out of the way and stared at us like they'd never seen two people say goodbye before.

"OK, Hols," Dad said, resting his hands on my shoulders. "I've got to go or I'll be late for work. Think you can find your classroom on your own?"

"I'll be fine," I said, noticing Dad's eyes had turned a little hazy. "You'll be with me all day, remember? In the Backpack of Cheer?"

Dad's thousand-watt smile was plastered across his

face but his bottom lip was quivering and his eyes were full of tears. I always thought parents were supposed to have it all figured out. He told me going to school would be the best thing for me, but now here he was, crying about it. I didn't understand. Isn't this what he wanted? Didn't he want me to spread cheer like him and Mum?

I waved him off and watched him disappear behind the school fence. After a few moments, my smile dropped. I waited a while, unsure what to do next. Everything felt flat, like the magic in the air had fizzled out. I wanted to call Dad back, to give him one last hug or wish him a merry day, but something told me not to. He was finding it hard enough to say goodbye as it was.

Instead, I yelled as loudly as I could, "DON'T FORGET TO SPREAD CHEER WHEREVER YOU GO!"

I waited for his response.

Nothing.

A bird took flight from a nearby tree and made the leaves rustle.

The phone rang from inside the school office.

Two ladies pushing buggies looked at me with startled expressions.

My heart sank.

Then I heard a stomping sound, followed by a car alarm. The tip of a red velvet hat appeared over the top of the fence, followed shortly by Dad's round face and infectious smile.

"LET'S SPREAD CHEER WITH A HO, HO, HO!" he beamed.

My spirits soared. He waved his hands above his head like those people that conduct airplanes down the runway.

I laughed. "Are you . . . standing on the car?"

He nodded. "Good cheer to you, Hols. Have a merry day!"

"Have a merry day, Dad!" I shouted back, grinning from ear to ear.

As he jumped off of the car bonnet, the school bell rang out. Groups of children were already gathering around classroom blocks that edged the playground and the caretaker was locking the gate. I stole one last glance at the fence in case Dad's head reappeared over the top, but all I heard was his rusty engine spluttering into life and his Christmas car playlist belting out into the street. I stood there listening to it grow fainter and fainter and fainter and –

"What are you waiting for?" the stern woman from the office snapped. "Get to class!"

I took a deep breath and followed the signs for Dickens Class. I was heading into the unknown, like Father Christmas flying his sleigh without Rudolph to light up the way. I pressed the button on the Backpack of Cheer and listened to Dad's voice one last time. It was fine. I was fine.

This was going to be the best first day of school ever.

MY BIG ENTRANCE

ickens Class was at the opposite end of the playground. I watched a trail of students disappear inside and felt a pang of nervousness in my belly. What would happen if I was late? Would I get in trouble? Would they even let me in?

I sprinted across the playground, my Backpack of Cheer bouncing up and down with such force it gave me a bit of motion sickness.

Mum always taught me to spread extra cheer if I thought I'd upset or disappointed someone. Like that time last July when I forgot to send Great Aunt

Agatha a Christmas card or when I accidentally used all of Dad's strawberry laces to knit an edible stocking for the postman.

I wondered how I could make it up to my teacher and new classmates for being late. I didn't have anything edible to give them and I certainly didn't have time to knit them a christmapology scarf.

By now I was so close to the door, I could hear them all chatting (probably complaining about the new girl holding them up), so I sort of panicked and did the only thing I could think of.

"Merry Monday, Dickens Class!" I sang. I pushed open the door, reached into pocket number twenty three of my Hollyhood and grabbed two handfuls of snowflake confetti. Then I pressed the button on my Backpack of Cheer so that Dad's voice burst into song, threw my hands in the air and wiggled my hips from side to side. The snowflake confetti fluttered around me like a miniature snowstorm. "I'm so sorry I'm late," I shouted over Dad's booming ho-ho-hos. "I'm new. Can I still come in? Am I in trouble? Should I do anything? I can sing you a carol?"

The whole class stared at me. The room fell silent. Even the teacher opened and closed her mouth like a goldfish. My mind whirred. Should I smile and wave? Was I meant to go round and shake their hands? Maybe I could show them my drunk reindeer impression?

"Ahem," the teacher coughed. "You must be Holly? Holly . . . Carroll?"

"Yes!" I nodded enthusiastically. "Some people call us the Christmas Carrolls. We –"

That was when I noticed it. My ears blocked the teacher's voice out as my eyes scanned the classroom. Where was the world map to track Santa's routes and delivery times? Where were the snow charts measuring the impact of climate change? Where was the Christmas tree to teach us about symmetry and ratios and weight? What about the circuit-board fairy lights? The elf portraits? The tinselibrary? Where was any of it?

"Holly, sweetheart," the teacher interrupted. "Why don't you find a seat and we can get properly acquainted in a moment? I'm just about to take the register."

I scanned the room. All eyes were on me as my head darted left to right. Every chair was taken. Every table occupied. Maybe I was supposed to stand at the back as punishment for holding everyone up for so long?

I turned to face the back wall and let out a sigh of relief. There was one empty seat on one tiny table in the corner of the room. A boy with messy blond hair and a loosely knotted tie was staring back at me.

"Archer," the teacher said. "Make some room for Holly please. You can be her first-day buddy."

The boy called Archer shuffled his chair away and stared at me with eyes so wide, he looked like

a traumatised owl. I blushed. I must really have
impressed him with my elaborate entrance.

Good one, Hols.

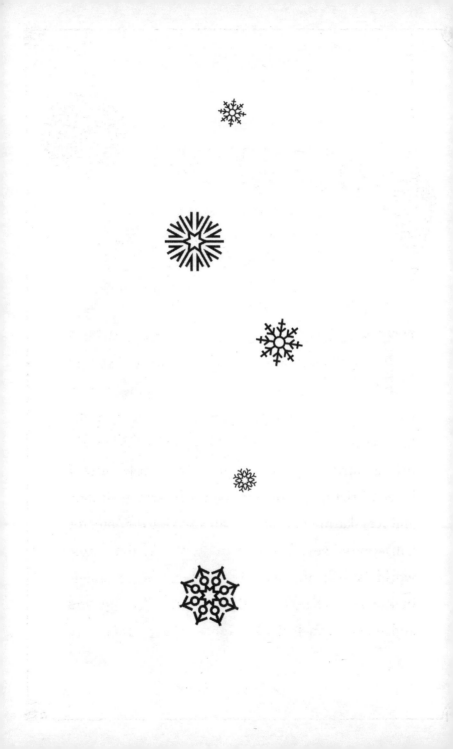

DICKENS CLASS

7

The class were as silent as snowfall as I walked to my seat. It reminded me a bit of Christmas Eve when you're lying in bed, listening for pattering hooves on the roof or the faint sound of jingle bells in the air. That's probably my favourite time of the year, you know. Sure, I love Christmas morning and Christmas dinner, and ice-skating and baking and decorating, but it's Christmas Eve I love the most. When the whole world is still and listening. When there's magic in the air. When that silence settles around you and makes you feel like right there, in that very moment, anything is possible. I –

"Holly?" the teacher said. "Are you OK?"

I shook myself from my trance and pulled my chair out. The boy at the table smiled weakly and looked me up and down. I beamed.

"You're Asher, right?" I said.

"It's Ar—"

"Ar? Like a pirate?"

Some of the students around us laughed.

"No." The boy's cheeks turned red. "It's Archer. Just Archer."

"Nice to meet you, 'just Archer'," I grinned. "What would you like for Christmas this year?"

The boy's eyes widened even more.

"OK, Dickens Class," the teacher said, perching on the edge of her desk. "Let's take the register and then we can move on to some start of term announcements. Holly?"

The class turned to look at me. *Again*. I felt as famous as Father Christmas.

"You're supposed to answer," Archer said under his breath.

This bit I knew already. I'd been practising my register-answering voice all week.

"I will," I said. "But doesn't she need to check it twice? Like Santa?"

The corners of Archer's mouth quivered.

"Holly?" the teacher said a little louder.

"Here!" I replied, waving my hand in the air and scattering a few leftover pieces of confetti above me.

The teacher's lips twitched. She seemed as excited as I was about the first day of school! Once she had taken the rest of the register, she adjusted her feathery auburn hair and clasped her hands in her lap.

"So, Dickens Class. Welcome to Year Five! My name is Miss Eversley. I know most of you know me already. We've got a big year ahead of us with lots to learn and some exciting projects, and I expect us all to help each other along the way. Do you understand?"

"Yes, Miss Eversley," the class chanted in unison.

I stared at them in shock. They were so in time, so in tune, so *rehearsed*. Maybe we could start a Dickens Class Christmas choir?

"Now, who knows why we're called Dickens Class?" Miss Eversley said.

A girl in the front row shot her hand up.

"Alice?"

"Because we'll be reading *A Christmas Carol* this term?"

Miss Eversley smiled. "Precisely. I –"

"YES!" I squealed. I put my hand up to high-five Archer, but he looked at me like I'd grown two heads. "That's my favourite book, Miss Eversley. That's my whole family's favourite. Thank you! Thank you!"
I high-fived myself so I didn't leave myself hanging. My stomach was tingling with excitement. I wanted to jump up and down.

Wait.

Why was I the only one clapping?

"While I'm thrilled with your excitement, Holly,"

said Miss Eversley, "we must try to keep calling out to a minimum, OK?"

I shrank back. Don't be late. Don't call out. Don't call Archer 'Ar'. I was learning so much already!

"Now, we won't be starting *A Christmas Carol* for a few weeks," Miss Eversley said. "First we need to go over some basic teaching and see where you're all at, and then we'll get to the exciting stuff."

That was why the classroom was so bare. They were easing us in gently.

"But before we can do any of that, we need to nominate our new class representatives," the teacher continued. "As most of you know, every class at Lockerton Primary has two class reps who meet with the head teacher once a month to talk about the school and some things they might like to change. It's a real honour to be named a class rep and the position should not be taken lightly."

The girls on the front table sat up a little straighter. They were grinning at the teacher like they were in some kind of smiling contest, so I followed their lead and shot Miss Eversley my biggest, cheesiest Merry Monday smile. It wasn't until Archer shuffled his chair away that I realised it was also the face I made when I had trapped wind. Great. I'd only been here a few minutes and I'd already shown everyone my confused fart face.

"Now this year," Miss Eversley said, "we'd like you all to apply. We're going to write some speeches, practise our speaking and listening skills, and really focus on how we can help the school and the wider community. In fact, if you become the class reps for Dickens Class, the first thing you'll be in charge of is our big fundraising event, which takes place every September. You must work out how we can raise as much money as possible and you'll decide who the money should go to and why. Who's up for the challenge?"

I jumped out of the chair and waved both arms above my head. "Oh, me, Miss Eversley! Me, me, me! Pick me. Pick me!"

The girls at the front of the room quietly raised their hands, but the rest of the class let out a dull groan. What was going on? Hadn't they been hanging off Miss Eversley's every word? Didn't they realise this was a chance to spread cheer?

Miss Eversley smiled and motioned for me to sit back down. "We'd like to get started on this activity straight away," she said. "The person sitting next to you will be your class rep partner. You'll be working on your speeches together and presenting your ideas first thing tomorrow. I'll pop some suggestions on the board for things you could talk about, but have a discussion with your partner while I do that and see what you can come up with yourself."

I turned to face Archer, a billion ideas already buzzing in my head.

"We've got this!" I said. "Why don't we . . ."

Archer's eyes were fixed on the wall beside him, like he was trying to avoid something.

I tried again. "Where shall we start, partner?"

I spread my smile as wide as I could and waved frantically with one hand.

"What are you doing?" he said.

"Spreading cheer!" I replied. "Obviously."

He did a little head nod thing as if to say, "Oh, right," and went back to staring at the wall.

"So, Archie," I said. "I mean, Archer. Personally I quite liked 'Ar'. Have you been a class rep before?"

"Class reps aren't really my –"

"What about the school itself? How long have you been here? Do you know much about it? I bet it's longer than I've been here. I've only been here about twenty-three minutes. Do you know all the ins and outs and secret hiding spots?"

He scooted his chair away, giving me a bit more room to squeeze my Backpack of Cheer and Hollyhood under the table. "Er . . . I suppose."

"So you know what people do to spread cheer around here? Do they have a Thankful Wall? Where's the Christmas card postbox? Why aren't there decorations in the trees yet?"

"You do know it's September, don't you?" Archer said quietly.

"What?"

"It's September. Why would the school have any of that stuff?"

"Huh?"

He stared at the Backpack of Cheer like he was trying to solve a really difficult maths equation.

"You don't . . . people don't . . . umm . . ."

I laughed. "Just tell me. I don't know how things work around here."

Archer pushed his hair out of his eyes and looked at me warily. I could tell he was trying to choose his words carefully. "Normally," he began, '"people don't –"

"Archer Edwards?" a voice shouted from the door. It was the woman from the office. "Come with me."

Archer slid his chair back.

"But what about our presentation?" I said. "I can't do it alone."

We looked at our teacher for help.

"How long will Archer be, Mrs Terse?" Miss Eversley said.

"How do I know?" the woman barked back. "I'm just a messenger."

Miss Eversley raised her eyebrows and took a deep breath. Even she could see that Mrs Terse could seriously do with some cheer in her life. My mind drifted to my arts and crafts cupboard at home and what I could make her in time for tomorrow. Some mistletoe earrings? An elf-control timer to make sure she got her paperwork done on time? Some personalised Tushy Tinsel with her face on it?

"I've got an idea, Holly and Archer," Miss Eversley said. "Why don't I arrange for you two to see each other after school? That way you can still take part in the presentation tomorrow."

Archer stopped halfway between the door and Miss Eversley and shook his head. "Miss Eversley, I –"

"Come to mine!" I said. "I can make some plans

for the presentation and we can practise in front of my mum and dad."

"Thank you, Holly," Miss Eversley said, nodding at Archer to leave with Mrs Terse. "I'll give you some prompt cards to take home, which should help you both, too."

My stomach lurched. "CARDS!" I shouted. "How could I forget?"

"Holly, dear," Miss Eversley said, her tone firm. "Do you remember what I said about calling out?"

I grabbed the Backpack of Cheer and slammed it on to the table, setting Dad's ho-ho-hos off again. I rummaged around inside, hearing the rest of the class snigger in anticipation.

"Ta daaa!" I sang. I pulled a stack of cards from the bag and ran across the room to Archer.

"What's this?" he said, turning the envelope over in his hand.

"A Christmas card, of course!" I smiled, pointing at the holly and berries I'd drawn on the envelope.

"To introduce myself to the class."

Archer looked from the envelope to me and back again.

"It's my first day Christmas card," I explained. "I've got one for everyone. Here, here you go, here's yours, pass them along . . ."

I ran around the room, handing them out and wishing everyone a merry Monday. By the time I got back to my desk, Archer and Mrs Terse had disappeared.

"Well then," Miss Eversley said, popping hers on her desk for later. "Thank you very much, Holly. Shall we get on with the rest of the session now?"

I sat back in my chair and smiled at my classmates. The day ahead felt so new and exciting, like opening a gift from Santa and not knowing what you might find inside.

We spent some time designing name tags for our pegs and bookmarks for our library books (I pulled out my own stationery supplies from the Backpack of Cheer, and even got a few oohs and ahhs from the class). Then we had a quick fire drill where we had to stand in the playground in lines and do the register again. It felt a bit more serious than the register we had done earlier, so I didn't bother waving my hand or spinning around, but I did wait for Miss Eversley to check the list twice. It was only polite.

"OK, Dickens Class," Miss Eversley said when we got back to the classroom. "Pack up your things and head out to break. We've got some spelling tests and a maths quiz lined up, just to see how much you've remembered over the summer."

Everyone grabbed their bags and ran out of the room before Miss Eversley finished her sentence. Behind them they left a few wonky chairs, some scrap pieces of paper and . . . oh.

Twenty-eight unopened Christmas envelopes.

CHRISTMAS HAD ARRIVED

8

I hadn't stopped thinking about the class rep speech all day. For the first time ever, I had an entire school to spread cheer to. That meant hundreds of children, plus their siblings and parents, and maybe their neighbours, and their neighbours' neighbours and their . . . You see where I'm going with this, don't you?

By the time I got home, the sun was so sizzlingly hot, I could've jumped into a pool of ice-cream and still have sweat dripping down my back. It was that kind of heat that made the air steamy and the ground feel like lava. It was almost unbearable, but between the sound of

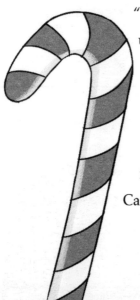

ice-cream van jingles and the smell of freshly-cut grass, arriving home to Sleigh Ride Avenue made all of the sticky, sweaty uncomfortableness vanish in an instant.

"Why?" I hear you ask.

Isn't it obvious?

Christmas had arrived.

Dad's homemade snow machines were shooting fake snow from the roof, the ten-foot candy canes we made last year ran all the way to the front door, and there were so many lights and strands of tinsel, it looked like the garden was glowing.

"Mum," I breathed. "This is –"

"Unacceptable," a voice spat behind us. "Completely unacceptable. It's an eye-sore, an abomination, a –"

"Mr Bleurgh!" I beamed, eyeing up his tweed blazer and matching bow tie for future fashionising inspiration. "This is my mum, Snow Carroll. What do you think of the –"

❄ 76 ❄

"*Snow?*" The old man scoffed. "Your name is *Snow*? What are you folks, some sort of travelling circus?"

"You might like to think of us as a circus of cheer, yes!" Mum laughed, producing some bells from her pocket and jingling them in front of Mr Bleurgh's nose. "What do you think of the Christmas lights, Mr Bleurgh? We'd be more than happy to decorate your house if you'd like a helping hand?"

Mr Bleurgh's face turned so purple, I thought he'd stopped breathing. It was actually quite impressive.

"And of course we'll invite you to our house-warming party in a couple of weeks' time," Mum added. "It's the first time we've had neighbours in years, so we'll be making lots of effort to spread cheer to each and every one of you."

"Spread cheer?" Mr Bleurgh grimaced. "House-warming party? Christmas lights?"

I was really starting to like Mr Bleurgh. He had a weird sense of humour, the most wonderful fashion sense, and he only ever spoke in questions.

"Is this some sort of joke?" he spluttered. "Are you people from another planet? Is my sister playing a prank on me? Will this all be gone by tomorrow?"

"Oh yes." Mum smiled, doing a little dance with her jingling bells. "You'll barely recognise the house by the end of the week."

Mr Bleurgh wiped his forehead with his hankie and pulled a small leather notebook from the lining of his blazer. "You do know you need to be approved by the Sleigh Ride Avenue committee before moving into this road, don't you?"

Mum and I exchanged befuddled glances.

"And I, being the longest standing resident of Sleigh Ride Avenue, am the founder and chairman of said committee," Mr Bleurgh continued. "So I must inform you that there are rules to be followed and regulations that must be adhered to. Are you aware you have already broken . . ." He stopped to consult his notebook. ". . . approximately one hundred and fourteen point five regulations and –"

"Won't you join us for dinner?" Mum shrilled excitedly, resting her hand on Mr Bleurgh's arm. "To go over the rules and regulations?"

Mr Bleurgh's eyes bulged. "I, er–"

"We could join the committee!" Mum gasped. "And help make the road more festive? In fact, we have big plans to make this the most Christmassy community the world has ever seen, and I think you are just the man to help us."

Mr Bleurgh puffed his cheeks like an angry frog.

"Madam," he retorted. "I most certainly am *not* th–"

"Snow!" Dad shouted across the lawn. "Where do you want this, Love?"

Mum let out a tiny gasp as Dad struggled under the weight of a giant light-up penguin.

"You found Porky!" she shrilled, running across the grass. "Just pop him down and we'll find a home for him. It was lovely to meet you, Mr Bleurgh. Do come back any time."

I fumbled around inside pocket twelve of my Hollyhood and pulled out a homemade Christmas cracker. "Merry Christmas," I beamed, straightening the crinkled edges and handing it to Mr Bleurgh with a flourish. "And thank you so much for welcoming us to the street!"

THE MORE THE MERRIER

9

Once Mum had found the perfect home for Porky the penguin, she led me around the newly planted fir trees and added dashes of silver glitter to the tops of the holly bushes.

"Holly," she croaked, her eyes dancing with Christmas magic. "Let's give ourselves a moment to take this all in. I don't think things can get any better than this."

My mind did that weird jump-flip thing, like revealing the other side of a coin (preferably a chocolate one). Surely this can't be, you know, *it*?

Yeah, it's incredible and everything – believe me, excitement was building in my stomach quicker than a nervous fart – but I'm only nine years old. Does this mean I've reached my peak before I've even hit double digits? Will life never be as exciting and beautiful as it is right now? What about when I design Santa's new suit at fashion school? Or I get asked to install the new Lapland Christmas lights? What about when I organise the Disney Christmas Day Parade?

No, Mum was wrong. The house might be gobsmackingly, mind-blowingly brilliant, but I had bigger and better plans than a few house decorations, and the class rep speech was the perfect place to start.

As we reached the front door (which had been painted a red brighter than Rudolph's nose), a car pulled up at the other end of the path. Archer and a middle-aged man wearing a straw hat and a bold Hawaiian shirt stepped out. Their mouths dropped open as soon as they saw the full extent of the house.

"Merry Monday, friends!" Mum shouted, waving

her arm above her head. "You must be Archer?"

Archer looked at the man, who I assumed was his dad, and remained close to the car.

"You've been busy!" his dad shouted, trying to take it all in. "You er . . . testing the lights or something?"

"Oh no," Mum said, her eyes wide at the thought. "Our decoration tests take place in April. We would never leave it this late."

Archer started saying something to his dad. His hands were flying about in the air and he was shaking his head, probably asking why they didn't test their decorations in April, too.

The man whispered something to Archer and then led him down the path, their feet crunching against the pebbles.

"You sure you don't mind us popping over like this?" he said, removing his straw hat to reveal a large bald patch on top of his head. "Miss Eversley thought it would be a good idea."

Mum beamed. "Of course not!" She unlocked

the front door and swung it open. "The more the merrier!"

The man stared at Mum like he was seeing a mirage. I admit, she was looking a bit plain today – not an inch of red or green in sight – but she was rocking the snowman look with her fluffy white apron, snowflake hair clips and huge yeti boots, and I thought it was a bit rude of him to stare.

"OK then, Arch," he said eventually. "Do you want to go inside?"

I grabbed Archer's hand before he could answer and yanked him inside. "Come on," I said. "We've got *snow* much to do."

"Bye Archer," the man shouted after us. "See you in a couple of hours!"

Archer looked over his shoulder like a lost little lamb, clearly still overawed by the decorations.

"Bye, Pa," he said. "Maybe make it an hour?"

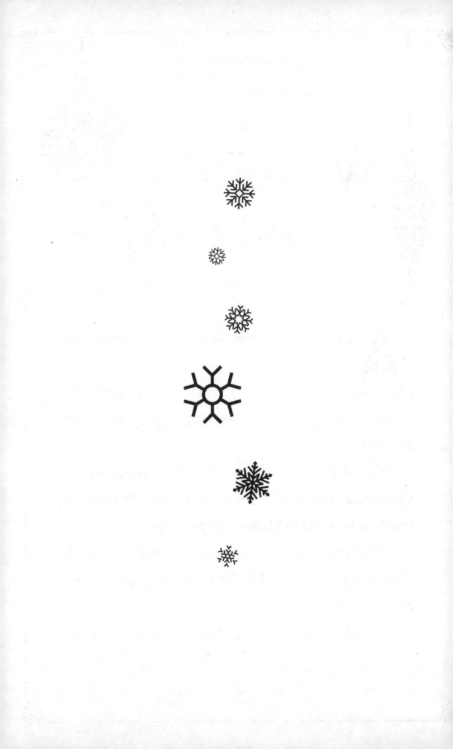

THE WRAPPING ROOM

10

"And here's the christmaloo that sings to you while you –"

"Shouldn't we be getting on with the speech?" Archer interrupted, checking the clock on the wall.

I looked at him curiously. I hadn't even started the Christmas tree tour or shown him our collection of two hundred and ten festive cushions yet.

"Why don't we go to the wrapping room?" I said. "We can plan our speech while I get some boxing practice in."

"You like to box?" Archer said, his eyebrows rising

so high, they vanished under his floppy fringe. "Like using punch bags and stuff?"

"No!" I laughed. "As in boxing up a gift."

"Oh." Archer followed me upstairs in silence, peering out of the window as he went. For someone who had just arrived, he seemed in an awful hurry to leave already. Then again, maybe that's what happens when you visit someone else's house. I wouldn't know.

"So," Archer said. "Do you mean you need to practise wrapping something in paper and sticking a tag on?"

"Boxing is more than just wrapping something in paper," I tutted, not bothering to hide how offended I was. "Just choosing the right kind of box is an art form. Didn't your parents ever teach you that?"

Archer shook his head.

"What about creating the perfect ribbon curl?" I checked. "Adding glitter to highlight the paper? Using real holly and ivy to decorate the top?"

Archer stared at me like he didn't know if it was a joke or not.

"It looks like we've got an exciting evening ahead of us then," I said, clapping my hands together. "Why don't you write down our plans for the speech and I'll demonstrate the steps to a perfect gift box."

"You really don't need to do that," Archer said, walking into the wrapping room after me. "I —whoa!"

I tapped the 'on' button on the festadio we kept by the door and it exploded with Dad's own rendition of the hearty classic, *Rocking Around The Christmas Tree*.

"This is . . ."

"Tinsel-riffic? Tree-mendous? Sleigh-perb?"

Archer gulped. "*Intense.*"

He took in the walls covered with rolls of wrapping paper and the reels of ribbon that hung from the ceiling like long curly pigs' tails. There were tables running through the middle of the room for sticking, stamping and adding sparkle, and Mum had naturally placed a Christmas tree in one corner so we could see how the presents would look underneath.

I smiled. "This room is Mum's pride and joy. She's

always wanted a wrapping room and sometimes she spends so much time in here, she forgets to go to bed. It's pretty snowtacular, don't you think?"

"Yeah." Archer paused. "I guess it is."

"So where should we start?" I opened the stationery cupboard and pulled out two gold clipboards, a giant sheet of card and some sparkly pens.

"I think I should be honest about something," Archer said, not knowing where to put his hands and eventually shoving them in his short pockets. "I don't usually apply for things like class rep."

"Why not?"

He shifted his weight from foot to foot. "It's just not my thing. Alice and her crew will get chosen anyway. They always do."

"But don't you at least want to impress the teacher?" I asked, totally befuzzled by his reaction. "Don't you want to spread cheer? Or share your Christmas spirit? Or . . . oh, my candy cane!" I yanked it from inside the lining of my Hollyhood and offered it to Archer.

"Er, I'm good, " he winced. "Look, why don't you give the speech on your own tomorrow?

You're the one with all the ideas anyway."

"I could," I said, my teeth sliding across the sticky cane. "But this is my first ever project, in my first ever school, with my first ever classmate. This means more to me than just a speech. After all these years of being homeschooled on my own, I was looking forward to doing something with someone, you know?"

Archer's face didn't move. I had no idea if my powers of persuasion (which once convinced our local cinema to play one of my homemade Christmas films for an entire month) were working.

"Pleeeeease?" I said. "You don't have to say anything. Just stand up the front with me and I can read everything out?"

Archer pursed his lips and looked out of the window. "You're not going to let me say no, are you?" he said at last.

I jigged along to the song on the festadio and grinned. "Nope. Come on. It'll be fun."

Archer rolled his eyes. "Fine," he said, sitting on

the floor opposite me. "But don't expect me to say anything. Public speaking isn't my –"

"Yes!" I cried, yanking a wobbly Santa-head pen from pocket number four of my Hollyhood. "Put it there, partner."

I had my hand stretched out, but Archer couldn't take his eyes off my Santa pen.

"What else are you hiding in there?" he said with a smirk.

It was weird to see him crack a smile. He seemed so serious, so wary of everything, but his smile softened his face and made his eyes light up.

"Oh, you know," I said. "Ideas. Secret inventions. Leftover Christmas pudding from last Sunday."

His smile widened. Should I tell him that I wasn't actually joking? The Christmas pudding was getting to just the right stage of staley crustiness, so that when I eventually ate it, I'd feel like I was saving it from certain doom. It would be an act of pure selflessness – a way of spreading joy to the poor old crumbly Christmas pudding.

"So I've been thinking about what we can raise money for," I said, eager to make a start before Archer changed his mind. "And I think we should raise money for the school itself. It's not the most joyful place to learn, is it?"

"OK," Archer said slowly. "What exactly do you have in mind?"

"That's where you come in!" I said excitedly. "I've been at school approximately six hours and twenty-one minutes, but you've been there way longer. What do *you* think they could improve?"

Archer shrugged, picking a pen off the floor and twirling it around his fingers. "I suppose the lunches aren't that great," he said.

I added 'lunch' to the left-hand side of my paper and started scribbling ways we could improve it on the right.

"We should give them my dad's recipe for the perfect gravy?" I suggested. "And his Christmas-tree cheese sticks. And the snowball sundaes and roasted chestnut crisps and cloudberry jam tarts. It's all delicious!"

"Er, OK."

"What about the school playground? Shouldn't they turn it into a Santa's playhouse with an ice slide and snow swings and a reindeer seesaw?"

"I mean, yeah," said Archer. "If you think that'll help."

"And we should start every day with Christmas carols, and the fire alarm should sound like jingle bells, and the corridors should be lined with tinsel, and we should have a Merry Moment of the Day where we all do one thing to spread cheer."

"Sure . . ."

"And we should send all of the teachers a Christmas card once a week and we should put on a Christmas show once a month – at least!"

"I think you might –"

"They should paint the school red!" I continued

excitedly. "Or make it look like a giant present. We could all write tags with our wishes for the world and attach them to the walls. Of course, we'd need to make sure the tags were waterproof and stuck on with some very solid superglue, but Mum's got tons of that in her studio and I'm sure she won't mind the school using it."

"I think they want to hear more about the lessons," Archer said, drawing on his hand instead of the paper. "You know, like things you'd change to help us learn?"

"You're right," I said, scribbling 'lessons' on to my piece of paper. "And I was thinking about that earlier. What do you think of an idea to take off ten minutes from all of our lessons and then spend that extra time at the end of the day on Christmas crafts? We could send letters to the elderly. We could make posters for the high street. We could make enough wreaths for everyone in town, I bet."

"Holly," Archer said seriously. "This is all getting a bit —"

"Invigergating?"

"Invigergating?"

I nodded.

Archer's eyes narrowed. "Do you mean invigorating?"

"Yes!" I said, clapping my hands. "That, too."

Archer continued to graffiti his wrists with my glitter pens. He may not have realised it yet, but we were going to blow Miss Eversley's socks off with our speech, and then we were going to become the best cheer-spreading class reps the world had ever seen.

"Holly?" Archer said, not bothering to look up. "How much longer will this take?"

CHEER-O-METER RATINGS

11

"Hollypops!" Mum called. "I've made ice cakes!"

"Where is everyone?" Dad's voice followed. "I'm ho-ho-home!"

Mum and Dad danced into the wrapping room, waving their hands to *Jingle Bell Rock*. Ivy wobbled in behind them, wearing a bright red T-shirt that said *SNOW BIG DEAL* across the front.

"Nick," Mum said, twirling through the ribbons that hung from the ceiling. "This is Archer. Holly's new friend from school."

Archer shoved his jittery hands in his pockets. "I wouldn't say we're –"

"Archer, my boy!" Dad smiled, holding his hand out and chucking some snowflake confetti in the air. "Merry Monday to you!"

Although Archer's long blond hair covered one eye, the other one flitted from Dad's face to his outstretched hand and back again. He looked startled, like a reindeer trapped in headlights.

"Yeah," he said, finally shaking Dad's hand. "Merry, er, Monday, Mr Carroll."

"Now, I've had an idea," Dad said, patting Archer on the back. "And I know it goes against tradition, but as we've all had such exciting first days, I think we should share our cheerometer ratings now instead of at dinner. What do you say?"

"I think that's snowpendous!" Mum beamed. "Can I go first?" She popped the plate of ice cakes (which most people call *rice* cakes, the weirdos), on the floor in front of us. "I think I would give my day an . . ." She tapped her finger against her chin, pretending to ponder her answer. "An *eleven*!"

"Out of ten?" Dad cried, spraying a layer of ice cake across the floor.

Mum nodded enthusiastically. "I've had the most magical day, darling. This house must've got my creative juices flowing, because I designed three new aprons, found some new material, and got in contact with some old suppliers in Japan who want to place an order. On top of that, I had the most wonderful cloudberry jam on toast this morning, and seeing all the work on the house come together has made my Christmas spirits soar."

"Bravo!" Dad said, sneaking another ice cake when he thought we weren't looking. "I would rate my day a nine out of ten. It was almost perfect, but it's always hard starting somewhere new, isn't it? The garden centre are making some nice plans for their Christmas market, but they're nowhere near as far along as they should be. I've made it my mission to add a Christmas tree farm and hang all the decorations out by next week, but they just keep saying they have a 'process' and that Christmas doesn't start for them until November!"

Mum gasped. I covered my mouth with my hand. Archer's forehead crumpled.

Dad smiled warmly. "It's OK, it's OK," he soothed. "That's obviously why they hired me. They need a little help in the Christmas spirit department and that's what they're going to get!"

I felt sick. Christmas starting in November? What monsters!

"What about you, Hols?" said Mum. "Tell us about your day."

"I'd give my day a . . ." I really didn't want to tell them about the Christmas card disaster. They'd be so disappointed if they found out I had failed to spread cheer doing something as simple as handing out some cards. "I'd give my day a solid nine."

"Only a nine?" Mum probed.

I nodded. "It's only day one. There's always room for improvement."

"Well put!" Dad smiled, offering another ice cake to Archer. "What about you, my boy? What's your cheerometer rating for the day?"

"Me?" Archer said. His cheeks turned as red as Ivy's T-shirt. " I don't know. Maybe a six?"

"A SIX?" Mum, Dad and I shouted.

"You poor little snow cone," Mum said, shuffling closer to him and wrapping her arm over his shoulders. "Whatever happened?"

Archer's eyes were wild with panic. "Did I say six? I meant eight."

"Why only an eight, my boy?" Dad said anxiously. "Can we help with anything?"

Archer looked so uncomfortable, you'd think he'd fallen down a chimney and couldn't get out. I had no idea why he was so quiet and jittery and could only rate his day a six out of ten. Why had his day been so awful? What had happened when he left registration with Mrs Terse? Was I failing at this friendship thing already?

"I know what will help you," Mum said, prancing out of the room.

Dad continued talking about the plants he'd seen at work and asked Archer if he had any plans for his winter garden. Archer shook his head and said something along the lines of his family not really having a winter garden, but thank goodness Mum came back in at that moment, because if Dad had heard, he might have had a heart attack.

"Here you go," Mum said, holding a box of mince pies and a card out for Archer. "Comfort food, courtesy of the Christmas Carrolls. There are some recipe cards in the box, too, so you can make warm cinnamon cream to go on top and our famous hot chocolate to wash it down with."

Archer looked concerned, like it was a big elaborate trick and the box might blow up in his face if he took it.

"Go on," Dad urged. "A present from us to you for helping Hols on her first day."

Archer smiled and took the box, studying the huge red ribbon and bow Mum had attached.

"See," I said. "That's why we have boxing practice. You never know when you're going to need to wrap an urgent present."

"Twelve point eight seconds is my record," Mum

said, pointing to a chart on the wall. "But Holly is going to overtake me soon with all the practice she's been putting in."

Archer held the gift like it was made of glass and could shatter at any moment.

BEEP! A car horn honked outside.

"I . . . I think that's Pa," Archer said, scrambling to his feet. "Thanks for having me, Mr and Mrs Carroll. Thanks for the rice – I mean ice – cakes, and the gift and the card. It's really nice of you."

"Any time, my boy," Dad said. "There's plenty more cheer where that came from."

THE CLASS REP SPEECH

I turned up to school the next morning with colour-coded flash cards, a whole bag of elf helper hats that Mum and I made from felt and spare apron material, and the stack of Christmas cards from yesterday that were still begging to be given out. Like any eager elf trying to make a good impression, I made sure I arrived extra early, had extra glitter in my hair and spread an extra wide cheer-spreading grin across my face, but none of that mattered when I realised that Archer was nowhere to be seen.

"Let's go to the next person on the list,"

Miss Eversley said. "We'll come back to you as soon as Archer arrives, OK Holly?"

I nodded, trying not to show my disappointment.

"So, first up today, we have Alice Coombes and Liena Chung," Miss Eversley announced. "You've got five minutes, girls. When you're ready . . ."

Alice and Liena sashayed to the front of the room with their heads held high and wide grins on their faces. They had made *Vote for Alice and Liena* badges and were sticking their chests out in case we hadn't noticed them already.

Badges. Of course. Why hadn't I thought of that?

"Hello, everybody!" Alice said, confidently projecting her voice. "We are Alice and Liena and we'd like to talk to you about why we should be the class representatives for Dickens Class."

"Firstly," Liena said, flicking her dark hair off her shoulder. "We want to raise money for our school dance club. We need new costumes and props, and maybe a guest choreographer from time to time."

"We also think members of the dance club should be excused from class once a week to practise their routines," added Alice. "So that we can put on the biggest end-of-term show you've ever seen."

"Furthermore," Liena said, turning her paper over with a flourish. "We'd like to organise a hair braiding day to raise money for my Mum's hair salon. We'd also like one wear your own clothes day every month (there should be a prize for the best dressed student from each class), and any money raised would go toward designing a new PE kit."

"As most of the money will come from the big fundraising event this September, we'd like to introduce a September Soirée at Lockerton Primary," Alice continued, pronouncing 'soirée' as 'soar-ray' and making out like it was some kind of fancy party. "The soirée will have music, dancing and entertainment, and even a photographer to take our photo."

"It's sort of like a mini prom," Liena said. "So we think we should have limos and long dresses and fancy food, and even proper invitations with our names in swirly gold writing."

"We'll be charging quite a lot for each ticket," Alice continued, "so that we can cover the cost of a DJ and decorations. But any money left over will go towards the local stables so they can buy a new horse for our horse riding lessons. Liena's dad made a projection chart to show how much we'd need to raise, and we've designed posters to show you our research."

Research. Badges. Projection charts. What next – an Irish jig? I hoped not. Surprise dance routines were *my* thing.

"And last but not least," Liena added. "We know this is something the entire school will agree with . . ."

They paused for dramatic effect, then both said at the same time: "If you name us your Class Reps, we will petition for no homework at weekends."

The class burst into applause. There was even a standing ovation. Everyone was whooping and clapping and causing such a commotion, Miss Eversley had to step in.

"Told you there's no point," a voice said in my ear. "They've been practising all summer."

"Archer!" I cried, jumping in my seat. "Where have you been?"

He slipped into his chair and glanced around the room. The rest of the class were squealing like a pack of excited elves at the thought of no homework at weekends. If this was their reaction to a change of workload, just wait until they heard the plans I had up my sleeve . . .

"We need to focus," I said, blocking Archer's view of the class. "Alice and Liena are good, but they haven't mentioned Christmas. Not once. With a few extra additions, I think we've got this in the bag."

"Look, Holly, I really think you should . . ."

"OK, Dickens Class," Miss Eversley shouted a third time. "Settle down. Thank you for your efforts, Alice and Liena. You raised some really wonderful points there."

 111

Alice and Liena sat back in their seats, smirking at each other.

"Holly and Archer," Miss Eversley said. "You're up."

I dragged Archer to the front of the room and shoved an elf helper hat on his head. He immediately took it off and let it fall to the ground. There was a smattering of laughter.

Good one! I thought. *Get them onside. Make them think we're a comedy duo.* We were going to nail this.

"Hello everyone, and a very warm Tremendous Tuesday to you!"

I began. "I'm Holly Carroll of the Christmas Carrolls, and this is . . ."

I glanced at Archer for his cue. He shuffled beside me, his eyes fixed on the ground.

"And this is Archer Edwards of the, er, Edwards family," I said. "You probably know him already."

I waited for some kind of reaction from the class, but two girls at the back were plaiting each other's hair and a boy at the side was daydreaming out the window. Miss Eversley nodded at me to continue.

"Firstly, we think that every day should feel like Christmas," I said with a smile. "We should be excited to go to bed each night, so that we wake up the next morning eager to see what the day will bring. We should do everything we can to spread cheer, not just to each other, but to other classes and our community. We should learn in a magical, vibrant environment that fills us with wonder when we walk through the corridors. For this reason, we think we should raise money to turn the school into a real winter wonderland."

I handed a flash card to Archer so he could read the next bit, but he was as rigid as a wooden nutcracker.

I cleared my throat. "This includes creating a new playground for the younger year groups to use. We should create a snowtacular scene with ice slides and snow swings to make sure their playtimes are filled with joy."

Miss Eversley pointed at her watch and circled her finger to tell me to keep going.

"And I think the school needs a complete christmafication with tinsel and trees and decorations all year round," I said a little quicker.

Alice and Liena looked at each other. It was a good sign. A nervous sign. They knew we were going to win.

"And we should send each other cards once a week." I brandished my stack of cards from my Backpack of Cheer as an example. "And start every day with Christmas carols. We could even visit the local care home and sing to the elderly to brighten their day. We should put on one – no, *two* Christmas plays a month, and wear only red and green at weekends."

"Is this a joke?" a boy shouted from a table in the middle of the room.

"No," I said, delighted I'd come up with some ideas that surprised them. "If we really want to improve the school, we should become the most Christmassy community in the world."

I paused for dramatic effect, just like Alice and Liena had.

Why weren't the class cheering?

I sped through the notes on my flash cards, wondering what else I could make up on the spot. "We could make Christmas stockings for children in hospital. We could make wreaths for the local shops. We could give out hot chocolate and mince pies at the supermarket. We could create a light show on the school roof to put a smile on everyone's faces as they walk past."

A few students started whispering behind their hands.

"There are small things we can do, too, like change the fire alarm to jingling bells," I went on.

The noise in the room grew louder.

"We can have Christmas dinner and figgy pudding every day."

Alice and Liena were smiling so hard, it looked like their cheeks might explode.

"We can have a Christmas craft club. My mum can teach us how to make Christmas aprons."

I heard a few muffled laughs. Archer was still staring at the ground, captivated by something on the carpet.

"The carpets!" I said. "The carpets can be changed to red and green. In fact, we can redesign the entire school so each classroom looks like a miniature grotto. Teachers can call us elves and we can learn how to make toys, how to properly decorate trees, and how to become expert present wrappers."

The laughter was building now. One girl even had tears running down her face. What was so funny?

Were they just totally delighted with my ideas?

"I think we should sit down," Archer whispered, his eyes pleading.

"But . . . but . . ." What was it that Alice and Liena said to get such a good reaction? "No homework!" I blurted out. "Just spreading cheer wherever we go and spreading cheer . . ."

The laughter was deafening.

"With a ho . . . ho . . . ho?"

"What's she going on about?" a kid shouted, laughing so hard I could barely understand him.

"Is she for real?" another added, giggling with the girls on the table behind her.

I looked at Archer. What was going on? Had I missed a joke? Did I have Christmas pudding stuck to my face? I shook my head helplessly and felt my bottom lip quiver.

Archer sighed. Slowly, very slowly, he took a tiny step forward and opened his mouth.

"I think you should listen to Holly," he said quietly.

The tears that were pricking the corners of my eyes retreated.

"You might not agree with all of her ideas, but at least she's trying to make a difference."

A quiet hush fell over the classroom. Everyone stared at Archer. Even Miss Eversley's eyes widened.

Archer coughed nervously. "That's it," he said. He walked back to his seat and found another spot on the table to stare at.

Miss Eversley led the class in a measly round of applause.

I gathered my cards and elf helper hats and rushed back to our table.

"Archer?" I whispered, trying to shake off the thumping sensation in my chest. "What just happened?"

TRYING TO SPOT CHRISTMAS

13

Mrs Eversley made us stay in at break time because she said she wouldn't tolerate outbursts and wanted to teach us the 'importance of respect'.

I found it all a bit strange, to be honest. Mum never told me off for talking when I was trying to learn. And she certainly didn't tell me to stop laughing if I was having a good time. Being at school was feeling more cheerless by the second, and I wondered whether it was really the right fit for me and my candy-cane-filled Hollyhood.

Once the last two people – Arun Talwar and

Charlene Yakob – finished their speech, the bell rang for lunch. Everyone immediately pushed back their chairs and tried to escape out the door.

"Wait a minute!" Miss Eversley cried, waving some slips of paper above her head. "I need one person from each duo to come up and vote for who they'd like to be the next class reps. Just put a tick beside the couple you'd like to vote for and then I'll announce the winners after lunch."

Archer was already halfway out the door. I grabbed his arm and pulled him back.

"Can you decide who to vote for?" I said. "You know everyone better than I do."

I crossed my fingers behind my back and hoped he'd say yes. If I was being completely honest (and I *nearly* always am), I hadn't heard a word of anyone's speech since ours. My brain had just replayed everything I'd said over and over and over again, trying to work out where I'd gone wrong.

"Yeah," Archer said. "OK."

He fought his way through the stampede of students scrambling to get out of the room and took a slip from Miss Eversley.

"Thank you," I mouthed.

He replied with a half-smile and then looked away.

I wasn't entirely sure what to do next. Yesterday I was invited to the Head Teacher's office for a New Students Welcome Lunch, but today ... nothing. There were no 'Please Stop Here!' signs, or arrows with the words 'This Way, Holly!' that pointed me towards the lunch hall. I didn't even have a reindeer leading the way, or a North Star guiding me home.

You know what? Santa sure knows what he's doing, doesn't he? He makes delivering presents all over the world look way easier than finding your way around a new school. Then again, I suppose he does have magic on his side. Some people have all the luck.

I walked around the playground, wondering whether school lunches were anything like the ones I had at home. I mean, obviously they wouldn't have a fireplace for two hundred of us to sit around (although maybe Dad could build one?), but surely they would pull crackers and tell jokes and wear paper crowns and exchange notes of cheer? At the very least, they must have festive place names for everyone and napkins folded into the shape of Christmas trees?

I stopped at the edge of the field and looked around. Every patch of shade was taken, even the bit at the back of the smelly toilet block, and there wasn't a single candle or fairy light in sight. All of the students were gathered in groups: some tackling each other to the ground, some arguing over who could sit beside them, and others kicking a ball into a net. It made zero sense. The closest thing I saw to spreading cheer was someone sharing a packet of crisps, and they were cheese and onion flavour, so they may as well have been sharing a bag of reindeer poop.

I did a lap of the playground, resisting the urge to press the button on my Backpack of Cheer and listen to Dad's comforting ho-ho-hos. I hadn't seen anyone else with a singing, light-up, oversized backpack, and although it was undubidedly one of Dad's greatest inventions, I was getting the impression that if you didn't have the same thing as everyone else you weren't a proper school student at all.

I walked past Mrs Spencer's office and peered in the window, wishing I could eat lunch with her like yesterday. It had only been me and some new twins from Year Two, but Mrs Spencer had listened to all my christmafying ideas and even gave us name tags and a map of the school. I must admit, it wasn't the greatest cheer-spreading I've ever seen – she didn't add any sparkle to our badges and the map didn't show where to go for mid-afternoon cookies and milk – but Mum had taught me to treasure every gift I receive, so I gave her a thank you hug just the same. (Note to self: hugging teachers *may* be frowned upon. Who knew?)

It occurred to me that a daily lunch with Mrs Spencer could really benefit students who were feeling lonely or a little down. I decided to add it to my list of class rep ideas as soon as we got back from lunch – but when exactly was that? At home, lunch finished once we'd rehearsed at least three Christmas carols and drunk the last of the cinnamon milk, but at school there wasn't a single hymn sheet or frothy mug in sight.

Just when I thought I couldn't feel any more lost, I walked back towards the playground and spotted something that made me feel like I was dancing in falling snow.

A Christmas card.

And not just any Christmas card.

A Christmas card I had handed out in class yesterday. And someone was reading it . . .

THE CHRISTMAS CARDS

14

"Archer!" I shouted. I waved my arms above my head and ran over to him, stopping short of chucking snowflake confetti around me to announce my arrival. He'd already seen that trick, and might get jealous if I did it again.

"Is that my card?" I said, making myself comfortable on the tarmac beside him.

He looked at me like I'd caught him snooping around Mrs Spencer's office.

"No," he said, dropping it on the ground. "Sort of. I found it on the . . . erm . . . yeah."

I picked the card off the ground and gently peeled it open.

To my new friend. I am overjoyed to meet you and cannot wait to see what adventures we have at school together. My name is Holly Carroll (of the Christmas Carrolls) and this year for Christmas, I'd like a sewing machine. What would you like? I'd like to invite you to our house-warming party on Sleigh Ride Avenue (the third most Christmassy road name in the world. by the way). where we can sing carols. make mince pies and play What's in the Stocking. It will be on Saturday 21st September – I hope to see you there! Thank you so much for welcoming me into your class. With oodles of festive wishes and good cheer. your new friend – Holly Carroll (of the Christmas Carrolls). P.S. Merry Christmas!

"You, er, like to make an entrance," Archer said,

dodging out of the way so I didn't whack him when I took off my bag.

"Mum always says the best kind of cheer is surprise cheer," I said. "The kind you don't expect."

"If you like surprises," Archer mumbled.

For a moment I thought my ears had failed me. Who on snowy Earth didn't like surprises?

I watched Archer open his lunch box and busy himself unwrapping his – oh!

"They're not snowiches?" I said, leaning over him to inspect whatever he was taking out of the shiny foil. "Where's the turkey? The cranberry sauce? The crispy stuffing? The Christmas shapes?"

Archer laughed. "It's just a sandwich. A normal jam sandwich."

"A . . . jam . . . sandwich?"

"Yeah, you know," said Archer. "Bread. Butter. Jam. It's pretty basic but it's my favourite."

"Is it cloudberry jam?" I said, excited that we were finding something in common. "From Lapland where

Santa lives? My mum orders the berries twice a year and makes her very own jam and candies."

"It's just jam," said Archer, lifting a sandwich to his mouth. "Plain jam."

" Where's your lunch card?" I said, eyeing his plain jam sandwich sasspiciously. "You can't eat without reading your card first."

"Er . . ." Archer cocked his head. "Pa must've forgotten it today."

I let out a breath I didn't realise I was holding. Thank Santa's beard! For a moment then, I thought he was going to say he didn't get a lunch card!

"Don't worry," I said, pulling my *'Tis The Season For Eating* lunchbox from my backpack. "You can share mine." I prized the lid off and handed him the sparkly silver card that was resting on top.

"*To our darling Hollypops,*" Archer read with an awkward grin. "*We hope you're having a Tremendous Tuesday and your speech with Archer goes well. We'll be thinking of you both and can't wait to hear all about it over dinner. We are so proud of you for handling the move to school with such optimism and grace. We know you're going to do wondrous things there, including spreading lots of cheer. We love you from head to mistletoe. Love from Mum, Dad and giggles from Ivy."*

"See?" I smiled. "Plenty of cheer to go around. And they send you well wishes, too."

Archer handed the card back. He looked a little shellshocked.

"You get one of those every day?" he said.

I nodded. "Drawings at breakfast, cards at lunch and crackers at dinner time. Why, what do you get?"

Archer shrugged. "Sometimes I get an extra apple if they're going off."

I threw my head back and laughed. He was joking, wasn't he?

"Do you want to swap snow – I mean – *sand*wiches today?" I said. "I've got the usual turkey, stuffing and cranberry, but I'd love to try your jam one."

❄ **129** ❄

"Er . . . Sure." Archer held his jam sandwich out and I grabbed it like it was the last cookie in the cookie jar.

"Cheers," I said, chucking him mine. "Tremendous Tuesday, Archer!"

"Yeah," he garbled, his mouth already filled with turkey. "Tremendous Tuesday. Oh . . ." he swallowed. "You can call me Archie, if you like."

"Not Arrrrr?"

He laughed. "No. At least, not in public."

I shot him my biggest grin and spread sticky jam across my teeth with my tongue. "This is delicious!" I said, licking the runny gloop from my fingers. "We should do this again. Tomorrow maybe?"

"Swap lunch again?" Archer said, pushing more bread into his already overloaded mouth.

I shrugged. "If you like the snowich, then yeah?"

Archer finished his last gulp and washed it down with a carton of apple juice. "Why do you call them snowiches?" he said. "Is it because they're cut into Christmas shapes?"

"That, and also my mum's called Snow."

"Your *mum's* name is Snow?"

This always got such strange reactions for some reason. "It's not her proper name," I explained. "She changed it when she went to university, and changed her hair colour to match."

"I didn't know you could do that," Archer said, taking an apple out of his lunch box and crunching into it. "What's her real name?"

I grinned. "That's the biggest secret of all. She won't even tell *me* that!"

Archer tilted his head to one side and looked at me like he was really considering changing his name. I hoped he wasn't going to choose 'Gladys'.

"I think I'd quite like a sandwich named after me," he said eventually.

"Well, why don't we do that?" I said, already making a mental list of all my favourite ingredients (cinnamon, white chocolate and chicken gravy, if you were wondering). "We can call them the Hollywich and Archiewich."

"Or the Holarwich if we made one together," Archer said.

My mouth dropped open. Making a snowich together? Like inventing with a friend? "That sounds better than ice cream on toast," I breathed.

"Do you always think with your stomach?" Archer laughed heartily.

His deep chuckles filled the air and drowned out the

footballers shouting from one side of the playground to the other. It was like he couldn't contain himself. Now he'd opened the laughter gates, he couldn't close them. Although it was nice to see a more carefree side of him, the sound of someone laughing at me (*again*) made my tummy go a bit wobbly.

"Archer?" I said, biting my bottom lip. "Can I ask you something?"

"What?"

My heart beat faster inside my chest. I felt like he was going to tell me something I didn't want to hear – like that recurring nightmare where my stocking is filled with coal instead of presents. But I had to know.

I took a deep breath and cleared my throat.

"Why was everyone laughing at me during the speech?"

THE NEW CLASS REPS

15

The bell rang and made me jump.

"Forget about earlier," Archer said, getting to his feet and chucking his apple core in the bin. "They were just over-excited."

"But Miss Eversley said they were being rude and disrespectful. What did she mean?"

I slung the Backpack of Cheer onto my shoulder and ran after him. "*Ho, ho, ho!*" the bag sang. "*Good tidings to you all. Ho, ho, ho!*"

I instantly felt myself relax.

"You, er, might want to leave that outside," Archer said, stopping outside the Year Five block.

"It's a bit big to fit under the table."

"But . . . but where would it go?"

"I dunno. On a peg in the corridor?"

"You want me to leave Dad outside on his own?" I gasped, stroking the straps. "Won't he get lonely?"

Everyone tumbled inside the classroom with their plain bags and perfectly combed hair. Archer was shifting his gaze from side to side as if checking no one was listening.

"I guess I could leave my bag with yours," he said at last.

"I'd like that," I nodded, ignoring the strange fluttering in my tummy. "Let me just say goodbye first." I pulled the Backpack of Cheer toward me and hugged it tight. "Don't worry, Dad. I'll be back soon."

I looked expectantly at Archer. His eyes were narrowed and his head was tilted to one side. He stood in silence, lines forming across his forehead, and then slowly, very slowly, he leaned forward.

"Laters," he whispered, hesitantly fist-bumping his bag.

"It's good for our loved ones – and loved things – to know we care, don't you think?" I said. Archer smiled awkwardly and then crept into the classroom, keeping his feet to the floor. He was good at this blending-in thing. It was almost like he *wanted* to go unnoticed, like he was trying to compete with Santa slipping in and out of houses on Christmas Eve.

"OK, Dickens Class," Miss Eversley said, sliding a round pair of glasses up the bridge of her nose. "Let's see who got the most votes and will be our new class representatives, shall we?"

Everyone shuffled in their seats. I leant as far forward as I could. Archer gazed at his favourite spot on the carpet.

"So, a few of you got one vote each. A very well done to Shelley Olsen and Marie Lopez, Lauren Piazza and Yolandé Hassan, Sophie Chandler and Daniel Smith, and . . ."

Just as she turned to the last slip of paper, a gust of steamy-hot air shot through the classroom and sent the slips fluttering to the floor. She bent down to retrieve them.

"Archer," I said. "What happens if we don't get any votes? What happens if everyone laughs again?"

"They won't," he said, not moving his eyes from the floor.

"But what if they do?"

"It's not a big deal," he hissed. "Just forget about it."

Not a big deal? *Not a big deal?* Becoming a class rep was a guaranteed way to become an important part of the school. To make a difference in the community. To impress Mum and Dad and spread cheer to the rest of the planet. It was my first step to becoming the greatest cheer-spreader (second to the big guy in the red suit, obviously), the world had ever seen.

" . . . and Holly Carroll and Archer Edwards," Miss Eversley said, popping her head up from behind her desk. "Let's give them all a round of applause."

My head jerked up. Archer grinned.

"We . . . we got a vote?" I whispered.

"Yeah," Archer said. "I guess someone liked it."

I looked around the room to see if I could spot who it was. "Do you think we should send them a thank you card?"

"It's just one vote," Archer said, lowering his voice. "Don't get carried away."

I nodded and added 'don't get carried away' to my mental list of things I should avoid doing at school. I wondered if I should add cartwheels in the classroom and sledding off the roof to the list, but there was no sign of *not* being allowed to do those things, so I didn't want to get ahead of myself.

"And with a whopping ten votes," Miss Eversley said, grabbing my attention. "Is . . . Alice Coombes and Liena Chung! Congratulations, girls. Come up and get your badges."

Wait! There were actual *badges*? Ones that Alice and Liena could wear all year to tell everyone that *they* were in charge of spreading cheer in Year Five? Talk about kicking a girl when she was down.

"Told you," Archer hissed. "There's no point trying to beat them."

Alice and Liena walked slowly back to their seats, milking their victory and waving to their friends at the back of the room.

"You might just have to settle for being a regular kid like the rest of us," Archer said.

"No way," I cried, fixating on Alice's badge and narrowing my eyes. "Their speech barely included any cheer spreading at all. It was all about *their* dance club, *their* horse riding lessons, and *their* mum's hair salon. A class rep should be someone that spreads cheer to everyone, not just themselves."

"But they got voted in," Archer whispered. "You can't do anything else now."

"I can!" I said, already forming a plan in my mind. "I'm going to convince them to let me become a class rep, too."

"And how exactly are you going to do that?"

"Isn't it obvious?" I said.

Archer raised his eyebrows.

"I'm going to knit them a scarf."

DIALLING DOWN CHRISTMAS

16

When the school bell rang at 3:15, I couldn't wait to be reunited with my Backpack of Cheer. I was desperate to hear Dad's cheery voice and my fingers were longing to get hold of the knitting needles I'd hidden in the back pocket.

Miss Eversley had some end-of-day reminders about reading logs and history projects, but when we were finally allowed out of the classroom, I ran past everyone, hurtled into the corridor and threw my arms around my bag.

"Oh, Backpack of Cheer!" I cried. "It's been far too

long. I promise never ever ever to leave you again." I hugged it tight and set off the ho-ho-hos.

When I turned around, I caught Alice and Liena staring at me. Instinctively, I thrust my hands inside my Hollyhood and searched around for a present.

"Er, what are you doing?" Alice said, apparently not appreciating my talent for locating presents in 2.5 seconds flat.

"I'm sure I've got a chocolate hiding in here somewhere," I replied, jumping up and down to loosen the contents.

"A chocolate?"

"Yes, a chocolate. People give chocolates to celebrate sometimes. Like at birthdays and Christmas and –"

"We know what chocolate is," Liena said, her top lip curling slightly. "But why is it in your hood?"

"Easy access," I said, sticking my tongue out as I teased my hands in and rooted around.

"Aha! Got it." I prized the melted chocolate and

presented it to them. "Congratulations on being named class reps! And Happy Christmas."

Alice looked disgusted. "Happy Christmas?"

"I don't understand what's going on," Liena said, looking at me as though I'd just pulled a tap-dancing elf from my ear. "Are you stuck in some kind of time warp?"

I smiled, confused. "I . . . I don't know what you mean?"

"This whole Christmas charade," Alice said. "What's it all about?"

"I'm really not sure what —"

"Holly!" Archer said, nudging Liena out of the way. "Shall we, er . . . talk? About that thing?"

I scrunched my nose. What thing? "Do you mean the Holarwich?" I said. "Do you want to make it after school?"

Archer's cheeks turned red. "Erm, no," he said. "But let's talk about it, yeah? Outside?"

"OK!" I said, excited to get started on our new

invention right away. "I'll talk to you tomorrow then, Alice and Liena?"

Before Alice could turn away, I grabbed her hand and placed the warm chocolate in her palm. "There's another present on the way, too. I just need to make it first."

Alice held the chocolate at arm's length, like I'd just handed her a dollop of melted poo.

"What did they say to you?" Archer said, dragging me down the corridor and out into the playground.

"They were saying something about that game, Charades," I explained. "Have you ever played it before? It's where you act out something and –"

Archer stared at me with worried eyes.

"What?" I said, feeding off his nervousness.

"I think I need to tell you something," he said awkwardly.

It took all of my strength not to press the Backpack of Cheer again.

"I think you should be careful what you say to people," Archer said. "About Christmas, I mean. They might not get the whole spreading cheer thing."

"Spreading cheer thing?"

"I mean, they might not understand your love for Christmas. You know?"

I stopped walking and stared at him. He could barely return my gaze.

"Everyone loves Christmas," I said.

It took him a while to answer.

"Not as much as you," he said quietly.

"Well, yes, I realise that," I said. "That's why we're called the Christmas Carrolls. But –"

"I think some people are a bit intimidated by how

well you spread cheer, that's all," said Archer. "They might look at you strangely if you keep wishing them a Happy Christmas or playing your dad's ho-ho-hos. I don't want to upset you, but I know what it's like not to fit into a new school, and I just thought that might . . . you know . . . help?"

My brain whirred like a snow machine running out of puff. "So you're saying that my love for Christmas is too much for people to handle?"

"I mean, kind of…"

"And that me spreading cheer is intimidating?"

"A bit, yeah."

"So what, I should just *dial down* the Christmasness?"

Archer looked at the cloudless sky, his lip quivering. "Maybe, yeah."

THE SURPRISE

17

The drive home felt strange and uncomfortable. Dial down Christmas. Archer wanted me to *dial down Christmas*? But why? And how would you even do that?

Mum was talking about snowfall and her new ice skates while I had sweat dripping down my back and my legs were glued to the cracked leathery seat. My mind wandered to thoughts of this evening's Christmas crafts. The schedule included designing cards, knitting bobble hats and stuffing snowman cushions, which I suppose was a bit strange given that the rest of the street would be running through sprinklers and sizzling sausages on the barbecue.

The whole thing made me feel a bit confused, to be honest, like that time my sled spun out of control when we went to Lapland and I spent the rest of the holiday with my head on a pillow, looking at the world sideways. Something – actually *a lot* of things – just didn't make sense. Like why no one else mentioned Christmas in their speeches when the whole point of being a class rep was to spread cheer. And why not one person, not even my teacher, wished me a Merry Monday or Tremendous Tuesday. And why we were the only ones to have our decorations up. Had the heatwave confused everyone? Didn't they know what time of year it was?

My mind whizzed back to yesterday. *You do know it's only September?* Archer had said, like I wasn't aware it was only one hundred and fourteen days until Christmas and time was running out. His dad had said something, too, about just testing the decorations. And Dad's boss had said Christmas didn't start until November.

A cold shiver ran down my spine.

That... that couldn't be it, could it? There couldn't be other people who thought Christmas was only reserved for one time of year?

As we pulled up outside our house my mind calmed at the sight of the lights and snow-covered grass, but a few questions still niggled at the back of my brain. Why hadn't we sung a single carol at school? Why didn't Archer have a Christmas card with his lunch? Why had no one else cheered when Miss Eversley said we'd be reading *A Christmas Carol*?

I hopped out of the car, oblivious to anything Mum had said for most of the journey. A group of people were standing on the opposite side of the road. They were licking ice-lollies and taking photos of our house on their phones. I didn't blame them. It was merrynifiscent! The ice rink was now complete and it looked like they'd added even more lights since yesterday. There was also a snow maze at the side of the house and my hobby trees had been placed around the entrance.

Whooooa. Hang on, hang on. You've never heard of hobby trees? They're one of my favourite things ever! We basically think about something I've learned or enjoyed over the year and design a whole tree around it. We usually build them in November, so we have a good ten months to plan and design them, and each year they get bigger and better.

My very first hobby tree was a sleeping tree, because my only hobby when I was a baby was ... you guessed it – sleeping! Mum decorated it with crescent moons, navy tinsel and twinkling stars, and

Dad installed a speaker underneath that played a lullaby every hour.

My second hobby tree was covered from root to tip in elves.

Elf pom-poms, elf baubles, miniature elf figurines, elf teddies reading elf books, and hundreds of tiny elf shoes tied together with string. Yes, I was obsessed with elves when I was two – they were my very first friends.

My third hobby tree was made out of wooden sleds, balanced on top of the other like a higgledy-piggledy game of Jenga. They were all covered in snow and fairy lights, and some had presents tied to the back with ribbon and bows. After that came the snowball tree (it was the first year I'd seen real snow and I was hooked from the first touch), then a ballet tree (I was determined to become a ballet dancer after watching *The Nutcracker*), and a giant book tree the year I learned to read.

In my sixth year we made a gingerbread tree. If I'm being totally honest, I think it's our greatest achievement. Every single layer was baked separately and then decorated and covered in a sticky see-through glue. It took an entire year to build, and Dad said one day we could make one that was bigger than our house!

After the gingerbread tree there was a memory tree, with photos and special objects attached from all the Christmases gone by, and then I had a fashion tree that was decorated with Mum's aprons and some of my favourite fashionised items –

"Holly?" Mum called, snapping me out of my trance. "Did you hear what I was saying? Do you want to see your surprise?"

"Surprise?" I ran forward to join her and Ivy under the candy cane archway. "What surprise?"

She laughed. "The one I was talking about the whole car journey home?"

I drew a blank.

"About the call your father had today?"

Er . . .

"About the delivery at the garden centre they refused to take?"

I did that nod-your-head-and-pretend-you-were-listening-to-every-word thing. "Oh yes, the delivery," I said. "What's it for again? Carrots for the reindeer? Mistletoe trees? Holly bushes?"

"It's something a little larger than vegetables and flowers, darling," said Mum. "Maybe it's just easier to show you."

She smiled and guided me around the side of the house. I couldn't see it clearly at first, but as we drew nearer, I saw eight wooden stables at the far end of the garden and huge stacks of hay forming four walls around the edge.

"Figgy puddings!" I exclaimed. "This . . . this can't be real, can it?"

Ivy waved her arms above her head and made a loud *ooooh* sound. She was wriggling so much, Mum could barely hold her.

"They're ours until we find a new home for them,"

Mum said, pushing a hay bale to one side so we could get inside the paddock. "And fortunately your father's herding certificate is still in date so they're allowed to stay here as long as they need to."

"But Mum!" I cried. "They're . . . they're . . ."

"Weindeer!" Ivy shouted with glee.

18 REGGIE

"Girls," Mum said, her eyes sparkling with Christmas joy. "I'd like to introduce you to the newest members of the family: Og, Grog, Fog, Sog, Tog, Pog, Cog . . . and Reginald."

A small grey donkey peered out from behind a reindeer's bum. He had a white patch around one eye, a pair of inflatable antlers strapped to his head, and he ran towards us hee-hawing loudly.

"I can't believe it!" I cried, wrapping my arms around Mum's waist. "We have pet reindeer? And a donkey?"

"Shhh!" Mum whispered, cupping her hand to her mouth. "This little fella thinks he's a reindeer, so don't say anything that might upset him. He's a sensitive soul."

Reginald ran circles around us, playfully nudging us with his head and proudly thrashing his inflatable antlers from left to right. After a few minutes he made himself so dizzy, he stumbled into a bale of hay.

"Hee-haw," he laughed.

Ivy clapped her hands and squealed in delight. Reggie was the most excitable, energetic bundle of fur she – no, *we* – had ever seen.

"Do you remember that farm we took you to a couple of years ago?" Mum said, popping Ivy on the straw-covered grass. "When I was pregnant with Ivy?"

I nodded. Of course I remembered it. I cried for days when Dad said we had to go home.

"Well, the farmer called your father because he remembered him saying he was a certified reindeer herder," Mum explained. "He told Dad that he was getting too old to look after the reindeer now and that he'd sold most of them to someone in Wales, but that he still had seven left and did we know anyone that would take them. We asked the manager at the garden centre, but he said their Christmas stables weren't ready yet, so your father did what I knew he'd do . . ."

"He offered for them to stay with us?"

Mum smiled. "Yes."

My heart felt like it might burst into song. I didn't know what to do first. Jump into the hay, bust out a happy dance or knit the farmer the world's longest thank-you socks.

"And what about Reggie?" I said, helping the little donkey out of the hay and tickling his nose. "He's not a –"

"Shhh!" Mum said as Reggie's ears pricked up. "Don't say it."

"He's not an *ordinary* reindeer," I said slowly. "He's extra special. I can tell."

Reggie batted his eyelashes and stuck his front leg out like a model posing on a catwalk.

"The farmer said he just turned up one day when he was a baby," Mum said, stroking his fluffy ears. "He must've walked for miles on his own, the poor thing. They tried to find out where he was from, but nobody claimed him. So when the reindeer welcomed him like he was one of their own, the farmer decided to make him his own stable."

"It's nice to know that other people know how to spread cheer, too," I said.

"The only problem was –" Mum looked at Reggie affectionately – "he didn't want to use it. According to the farmer, he wanted to spend all his time with the reindeer. He ate with them, played with them and even wanted to sleep in the stables with them. He's got a bit of a limp and a wonky eye, but the farmer said he's a happy chappy most of the time. They say he's happiest when he's got his own pair of antlers. He feels like one of them, you know."

Ivy was trying to crawl up Reggie's leg, so I picked her up and let her stroke the fur on his back.

"I love him!" I smiled, feeling tears well behind my eyes. "Hello Reggie. That's a mighty fine pair of antlers you've got there. I bet they can make you fly really high on Christmas Eve?"

Reggie buried his head in my armpit and made a soft braying sound.

"We should get the christmacam," Mum said. "Your father won't want to miss this!"

She ran inside with Ivy and left me to play with Reggie and Og, Pog, Dog, Log, Bog . . . I feel like I'm getting some of these wrong. Reggie followed me everywhere I went and nudged my hand with his head whenever I stopped stroking him. Once or twice he fell into a daydream, and when he woke up, he dashed across the paddock to find me. It turned into a full-on game of hide and seek, and one time he spotted me, he nearly sent me rolling into the reindeer like a bowling ball crashing into skittles.

After a while, Mum came back out, pushing Ivy in a wheelbarrow filled with fresh hay.

"It's Reggie's dinner time," she called.

But Reggie wasn't interested in dinner. He only wanted to play with me and Ivy. Every time we tried to stroke a different reindeer, he butted them out of the way and cocked his head so Mum could take another photo. He was a camera-hogging, attention-seeking, reindeer-wannabe with an attitude, and we fell in love with him instantly.

We played with Reggie for what felt like hours, and when Dad came home, he set up a picnic in the paddock so we could eat dinner and pull crackers and wear paper hats with our new family members. It was one of the most magical nights of my life and I couldn't believe Reggie and the reindeer were ours.

"So, Snowflake," Dad said, spooning an extra helping of apple sauce on to my turkey. "How did your speech go with Archer? What's your cheerometer rating for the day?"

I pursed my lips and looked up at the darkening sky. All the feelings of worhusion (worry mixed with a bit of confusion) were fading away with the sunset. I suddenly felt more sure of myself, more confident, more like 'Holly Carroll of the Christmas

Carrolls' than I had in a while.

"I'd give my day an eight," I said.

"Only an eight?"

I nodded. "But tomorrow is going to be a ten. I can feel it."

Reggie rested his head on my shoulder as I ate. The students at Lockerton Primary might not be used to spreading cheer, but that's why joining the school was going to be one of my greatest achievements.

After all, did I want to be a reindeer that followed the crowd, or did I want to be a diva donkey with a taste for the limelight and a talent for spreading cheer? It was a no-brainer. Reggie had become my muse and inspiration. And if I brought as much Christmas joy to Lockerton Primary as he had to me, I'd be happier than Dad on a snow day in July.

Right, Dickens Class, I thought to myself. It was time for me to christmafy Lockerton Primary School, and nothing and nobody was going to stop me. I was going to start right away . . . After I'd made a *Reggie Is My Idol* badge, obviously.

LOCKERTON PRIMARY'S FULL OF CHEER

I pressed the button on my Backpack of Cheer twenty-eight times before the head teacher pulled me into her office. Everyone was looking at me. Some kids even pointed from the other side of the playground. Reggie would've been so proud.

On the twenty-sixth time I pressed the ho-ho-ho button, I did a little twirl to really show off my fashionising efforts. The glittery pom-pom snowballs on my dress fanned out and hit a few people as they walked past. (Don't worry, they were only made from cotton-wool balls. One time, a few years ago,

Dad let me use real frozen snowballs from his special collection in the freezer, but they turned out to be so heavy, the fabric on my outfit split in two, and by lunchtime it just looked like I'd wet myself. It wasn't quite the look I was going for, but I think I styled it out.)

As I spun and galloped through the school gates, everyone stared at the reindeer stickers I'd stuck to my collar and the flashing lights I had sewn into the seam of my dress. And although I didn't have a class rep badge like Alice and Liena (yet!), the *I love Santa* emblem I'd stuck on my dress pocket really made the outfit pop. Of course, I also wore my favourite snow socks and tinsel headband, and hid my knitting needles and wool inside my Hollyhood. Mum had even let me borrow one of her fluffy apron petticoats so that my dress stuck out like one of the ballerinas from *The Nutcracker*. I was tempted to wear a pair of inflatable antlers like Reggie, but that would have overdone it, don't you think?

On the twenty-seventh time of pressing the ho-ho-ho button, I realised I'd forgotten to take a photo of my new school outfit on the christmacam and wondered whether I had time to nip back home. Then the bell rang, and that was when I pressed the button for the twenty-eighth time and Mrs Spencer rounded on me quicker than you could say Rudolph The Red-Nosed Reindeer.

She whisked me into her office with kind eyes and a firm tone and asked me to take a seat.

Was this it? Was she about to say the school had made a silossal (both silly and colossal) mistake and actually they needed me to lead the way and be the Head Elf – I mean, class rep?

"Miss Carroll," said Mrs Spencer, sitting opposite me and taking a swig of a lemony-smelling tea. "Is there a reason you're dressed like that?"

"I'm spreading cheer, Miss," I said, reaching for the button on my backpack again. "And speaking of spreading cheer, I've made up a new carol for the school. Do you want to hear it? It goes like this. *Lock-er-ton Pri-mar-y's full of cheer. Lock-er-ton Pri-mar-y has no fear. Lock-er-ton Pri-mar-y keeps loved ones near. Lock-er-ton Pri-mar-y loves reindeer –*"

"Miss Carroll, I really think –"

"KEY CHANGE! *Lock-er-ton Pri-mar-y's full of cheer. Lock-er-ton Pri-mar-y has –*"

"Thank you, Holly. That's enough."

My voice faded out. I cleared my throat. Mrs Spencer rested her finger on her temple.

"Whilst I appreciate your efforts in preparing for school, Holly, unless we are dressing up for a school play or for show-and-tell or to raise money for charity, I'm afraid we must stick to a strict dress code," she said. "This consists of our approved uniform, black shoes and hair tied back. Do you understand?"

My head nodded, but it was lying. How could some stickers and cotton-wool balls cause such an issue?

"Let's remove the extra trinkets and I'll keep them here until the end of day, OK?" Mrs Spencer held her hand out and waited for me to start unpicking.

I hated that she called them 'trinkets' – like they were just regular objects without any feelings. Didn't she know when you make things with time and care, those items get a bit of your love trapped inside them? That's why Father Christmas insisted on making everything himself, you know. Until the world became so popularted . . . popurated . . . pooputated . . . argh, what's the word? Populated! Yes, until the world got so *populated* he could no longer make enough toys on his own, so then he asked the elves (who are known for having enormous amounts of love to give) to help him. That's why Mum makes all her aprons from scratch. No machines. No fancy computers. She always says all she needs is her two hands, a few ideas and a whole load of love. And that's why I make everything myself, too. I like to have a connection with the clothes I wear and the toys I play with. It's like they can hear my thoughts or know how I'm feeling. It's like always having a friend nearby.

"A little quicker please, Holly," said Mrs Spencer. "I don't have all day."

Honestly. This woman was snow joke.

Some things were easy to take off, like the headband and snow socks. Others, like the stickers and pocket emblem, took longer. I put them one by one into Mrs Spencer's hand.

"Your backpack and hooded scarf don't really follow protocol either, Holly."

My eyes widened. No. No way. Not my Hollyhood and Backpack of Cheer. They were as much a part of me as the spot on my bum.

"But I can see how much you treasure them," Mrs Spencer added. "So if you give me everything that's hiding inside the scarf pockets and you agree not to set off the ho-ho-hos, I'll allow you to keep them. How does that sound?"

Awful! Stupid! Soul destroying!

I took a deep breath. "Yes, Mrs Spencer."

Mrs Spencer nodded. "Good. Now, I've kept you long enough and you've missed registration. Sign in with Mrs Terse at the office and then run along to your first lesson. What have you got this morning?"

"PE," I said, feeling more and more deflated with every item I put into her hand.

"Right then. Leave these bits here and go and get changed. I'll keep your trinkets safe for you."

Mrs Spencer opened a drawer in her desk and dropped everything inside. She didn't even let me say goodbye. Then she led me to the door and watched me walk to the end of the corridor.

"Hurry along. Don't be late," she called after me, when *she* was the one who'd been holding me hostage this entire time.

When I finally reached the changing rooms, I changed into my sports kit and looked at my reflection in the smeary mirror above the sink.

I was sweating so much my skin sparkled and my curly hair had grown to twice its size. Luckily, my knitting needles were still hiding inside my Hollyhood, but my eyes were sparkle-less and I had zero energy to take part in whatever sport Miss Eversley was about to make us play. I didn't know how my day had gone downhill so quickly.

I slipped on my glittery red elfsolls, my tinsel bandana and *THERE'S NOTHING LIKE A GOOD RUN-DEER* T-shirt, and forced a smile across my face.

Nothing and no one was going to ruin my cheer today.

JINGLE BELL RUN

The rest of Dickens Class were already on the field when I ran out to join them. The bells on the end of my elfsolls tinkled every time they hit the ground, so I leaped and hopped in a quick-quick-slow rhythm to see what tunes I could play. It was only when I got closer and stopped to push my hair out of my eyes that I realised I'd made yet another mistake.

"Holly," Miss Eversley called, her eyes dropping to my shoes. "Those are some very, ummm, *unusual* plimsolls."

Plim-what?

"And I see you haven't had a chance to get a proper Lockerton sports kit yet, but that's OK," Miss Eversley went on. "What you're wearing is fine for today. Why don't you join Arun's team for a quick warm-up lap and then we'll do a few throwing and catching exercises, followed by a game of rounders."

I lifted my hand to my forehead and squinted into the sun. Arun's team were already halfway around the field. Even with my best half-skip, half-slide run that made me look like a penguin with hiccups, I'd never be able to catch up with them!

"Take a shortcut if you need to," Miss Eversley said. "I'll turn a blind eye just this once!"

I wished I could bust out a thank you dance for the nicest teacher I'd ever met, but there was no time for that. Instead, I thundered after Arun, my elfsolls hitting the ground with such force, the bells made it sound like a sleigh was flying overhead (I obviously looked up just in case).

"Doesn't she know how weird it is?" I heard

someone say as I finally came up behind them. "It's like she's two years old and doesn't know how to dress herself."

What was she talking about? Was my top on back-to-front?

"It's so unfair. Why does Miss Eversley let her wear her own clothes and not us?"

These were my running clothes. Seriously, what was the big deal?

"I don't think I'd *want* to wear that. Would you?"

Rude.

"I don't know. I thought the top was kind of cute."

I liked her.

"But only as pyjamas. I wouldn't actually wear it in public."

Oh.

"Does she really think it's Christmas every day? Are we meant to go along with it?"

Go along with what?

"She's not hurting anyone. She's just a bit . . .

what's the word? Eccentric?"

I think she meant 'ecstatic'.

"There's eccentric, Charlene, and then there's being on another planet."

"She hasn't been to school before, though. Maybe she doesn't know how it all works."

"I heard her family are exactly the same. I heard they sleep in igloos."

Igloos?

"I heard they have so many lights decorating their house, you can see it from space!"

Wow. Really?

"I heard they have a pet polar bear."

That's not a good idea.

"I heard they're so annoying, one of their neighbours is starting a petition to get them removed from the street."

Enough was enough. I opened my mouth.

"SORRY," I said. "WHAT?"

21 UNWELCOME

I went through the morning in a daze. I don't know how I muddled through rounders, but after offering to return the equipment to the PE shed, I barely had enough time to get changed before our music lesson.

When I finally squeezed into the tiny room filled with keyboards and a dusty drum kit, there was only one seat left at the very back, in the corner, opposite Archer. Normally I hated being so far away from the action, but the window beside me occasionally allowed a sliver of a breeze to pass through, and the view was perfect for daydreaming.

While everyone chose an instrument and played something they remembered from last year, my thoughts drifted to the comments the class had made during PE. I was from another planet. I was weird. I was electric (or was the word 'eccentric'?). I didn't know how to dress myself.

Knots in my stomach tightened like tangled tinsel, and a lump the size of a small bauble filled my throat. Why did nobody understand the power of spreading cheer? Why didn't they understand the real purpose of Christmas? Why didn't they understand *me*?

And then there was the worst comment of all, the one that had floated around my head like a snow cloud threatening to burst all morning. Someone wanted to remove us from Sleigh Ride Avenue. I thought about Mr Bleurgh and all the comments he made about our house and moving into the street, but they had just been jokes . . . hadn't they? Nobody would actually kick a family out of their new house because of a few flashing lights. Right?

I didn't know what was worse: feeling unwanted on Sleigh Ride Avenue or feeling unwelcome in my new school. I gazed out of the window, willing myself not to cry and thinking about what Father Christmas might do in my situation. I mean, if he can make billions of toys every year and deliver them all in one night, surely I could get Alice and Liena to like me, become a class rep, and help old Mr Bleurgh find his Christmas spirit? All I had to do was *spread cheer wherever I go and keep spreading cheer with a –*

"Holly?" Miss Eversley coughed. "Are you with us?"

"HO, HO, HO!" I said, finishing my thought out loud.

The class sniggered.

"Sorry," I smiled sheepishly. "Yes."

"Can we hear your song please?" asked Miss Eversley. "What have you chosen?"

I picked up a recorder and played *The Twelve Days of Christmas*. Miss Eversley stopped me when I got to 'seven swans a swimming' and asked me to choose a shorter song next time – like there was some kind of time limit on spreading cheer.

I went back to staring out of the window. Couldn't I do anything right in this town? It was like I was a broken toy that nobody wanted to play with. Despite trying to make myself as happy and shiny as possible, all anyone wanted to do was leave me outside in the snow.

I took a few deep breaths and rooted around for the elfipop (elf lollipop) I'd lost in the depths of my Hollyhood. It was only then that my fingers grazed the knitting needles and wool I'd shoved in there earlier, and my heart jolted with joy.

Friendship scarves. That was it! Once I made the friendship scarves for Alice and Liena, they'd understand the art of spreading cheer and would let me help them with their big September Soirée. Then Mr Bleurgh would see how much I was helping the community and he'd be so glad we moved into Sleigh

Ride Avenue, he'd give Mum and me the position of Head Elves – I mean, Chief Committee Members, and we'd be well on our way to making Lockerton the most Christmassy community in the world.

That was it, wasn't it? The answer to everything. A bit of wool, some dedicated craft time and a bucket load of . . . persilveeranse? Personverance? Sorry, folks, give me a mo . . .

PURSE-SIR-VEER-ANCE.

Nailed it.

THE MAGIC OF SPREADING CHEER

A t the end of class, we filed out of the room and into the steamy midday sun. Archer was already sitting in our lunch spot, staring at his sandwiches in disappointment.

"Don't start without me," I shouted. "Aren't we swapping again?"

He looked up at me with a sweaty brow and big, round eyes. "I thought you wouldn't want to speak to me again," he said.

"What? Why?"

"Because of what I said yesterday. About dialling down Christmas. I was only trying to help. I didn't want you to feel left out. I thought I had upset you. I thought –"

"Don't be ridiculous!" I cried, sitting opposite him and yanking my knitting needles and wool from my hood. "You were only trying to help."

"So you haven't been ignoring me all morning?"

"No. I've just been thinking," I said. I inspected the end of my knitting needles and sent them some telepathic messages about all the hard work they had ahead of them. "Do you know what?" I said, spitting in my hand and running the needles through it to clean them. "I actually think I've learned more about myself from being at school than I've learned about anything else. Is that meant to happen?"

"I dunno," Archer said. "Maybe."

I closed my eyes as I tried to make sense of my thoughts, but they were more tangled than the ball of wool I was holding. I thought about my next question carefully.

"Archie?" I said. "Do you believe in magic?"

"Er, what kind of magic?"

"You know. . . Christmas magic. The kind you can feel, but not always see."

He looked at me as if he was trying to work out the answer I wanted to hear. "I dunno," he said eventually. "Do you?"

I crossed my knitting needles over each other and wound the wool around the top. It took me a moment to get my rhythm, but soon the needles were click-clacking together and I didn't need to look at what I was doing.

"Yes," I said, wishing I was in an igloo or sitting beside a roaring fire. "But I think I'm learning that other people don't. People here don't see the magic in front of them. They don't hear the wonder in the air or taste the love that's gone into the food they eat. They don't get that tingly feeling in their tummies when someone smiles at them or feel the rush of energy when they make someone laugh. It's only a small form of magic. It's not like Santa's ability to pause time so he can travel all over the world in one night or anything. But it's magic all the same."

Archer didn't move. I couldn't even hear him breathe.

"Are you there?" I said. "Have I freaked you out?"

He laughed. "No. It's just . . . it makes sense. Like spreading cheer is magic."

I dropped my needles. "You get it?" I said. "You actually get it?"

Archer shrugged. "Maybe I'm beginning to."

We sat in silence for a while, occasionally grinning at each other as my hands worked at the speed of light.

"What are you making?" Archer said, leaning so far forward, his nose almost touched the tips of the needles.

"Friendship scarves," I said,

looping the wool over one ear and sticking my tongue out in concentration. "For Alice and Liena."

"Because you think they'll make you a class rep?"

"Once they hear my ideas and see their scarves, yes."

"But how will a scarf change their mind?"

"Once I spread cheer to Alice and Liena, they'll spread cheer to someone else," I said. "And then that person will spread cheer to others, and so on and so on, forever and ever, all over the world, until it eventually comes back to me and the whole world will be . . ."

"Cheerful?"

I nodded.

"And all of that will come from you giving Alice and Liena a scarf?"

"It's a start, isn't it?"

Archer's forehead crinkled. "I suppose."

It was almost the end of lunchtime by the time I remembered the surprise I had for Archer.

"Oh!" I cried. "I've got something for you."

"For me?"

I slid the Backpack of Cheer closer to him. "Look inside my lunchbox."

Archer hesitantly reached inside and popped the lid open. His eyes widened.

"There's two sets of snowiches," he said. "And two cards!"

"One for me and one for you," I said. "But we don't have to read them now if you don't want–"

Archer fumbled with the golden envelope, yanked the card out and whizzed his eyes across the page. Gradually, his expression changed from surprise to intrigue to . . . what was that, *gas*? Eventually he looked at me with wide eyes.

"Who's Reggie?" he said, scanning the card again. "And what reindeer?"

I took my needle away too quickly and dropped a stitch. "Archie?" I grinned from ear to ear. "What are you doing after school?"

BEST FRIENDS

23

I sat on the front step of our house, scoffing a mince pie and adding a few more rows to the friendship scarves. They were coming along rather nicely. Green and gold for Alice, and red and silver for Liena. I even had a bag of light-up pom-poms to add to the bottom.

"You know you look like an eighty-year-old grandmother?" said a voice.

I jerked my head up. Archer was grinning at me. To be fair, I could only just see over the wall of wool I'd built, and I was wearing Mum's old reading glasses because they were in the shape of crescent moons and made me look like Mrs Claus. She's my ultimate fashion guru, you know.

"You took your time," I said, brushing the bundles of wool to one side and getting to my feet.

"Pa made me do my homework first. Sorry."

It was the first time I'd seen Archer out of his school uniform. He was wearing a faded red T-shirt, brown shorts and green stripy socks. I'd never seen him so colourful, and although he could still do with some glitter or bells, I appreciated the effort.

"We'll turn you into a Christmas Carroll in no time," I said with a smile.

Archer chewed his cheek like he was trying really hard not to smile back. "Well?" he said. "Where are these reindeer then?"

I chucked the friendship scarves over my shoulder and the bag of pom-poms under my armpit, and walked Archer round the side of the house.

"Now don't let Reggie scare you," I said. "He's a little —"

WHACK!

Archer fell to the ground like a sack of presents as Reggie barged into him.

"Reggie!" I cried, trying to pull him away. "How in the North Pole did you escape?"

Reggie licked Archer's nose and tilted his chin from side to side, displaying his inflatable antlers proudly. Then he dug his head into Archer's chest and stayed there, letting his tongue roll out and a pool of slobber sink into Archer's T-shirt.

"*This* is Reggie?" Archer laughed, scratching him behind the ears. "A donk—"

"—deer!" I shouted. "The most special in all the land."

Reggie reversed and looked at Archer with teary eyes and his tongue hanging down to his chin.

"Call him a reindeer," I hissed. "Quick, before you upset him."

"Er . . . you're a reindeer?" said Archer.

Reggie's head lifted a few inches higher. He displayed his wonky teeth in the widest, crookedest, cheesiest grin I've ever seen.

"Reggie," I said, patting him on the back. "Meet Archer Edwards of the Edwards fam—"

"Archie is fine," Archer said.

"OK then. Meet Archie. My best friend."

Archer did one of those weird double-take things, like he wasn't sure if he heard me correctly.

"Best friend?" he said.

Oh. Had I left it too late to ask him? "Yes," I said cautiously. "Aren't I yours? We've eaten lunch together twice."

He shoved his hands inside his short pockets.

"Yeah," he said after a moment. "I suppose so."

Reggie must've sensed the awkwardness because he nudged us with his head all the way to the paddock at the far end of the garden. "Holly," Archer breathed, staring at the stables with wide, disbelieving eyes. "You have seven –"

"Hee-haw!"

"Sorry – *eight* – reindeer in your garden. Where did they all come from?"

We found a corner of the paddock that wasn't filled with donkey poo and made ourselves comfortable. Mum had left us fleecy blankets and a flask of hot chocolate, but Archer said he'd need an ice bath if he got any hotter. Instead, Reggie slumped down beside us and plonked his head on Archer's lap. Like *that* would cool him down.

We sat there for ages, Archer stroking Reggie's ears and me furiously looping stitch after stitch and telling Archer about the reindeer. Gradually, as the sun went down, the air cooled by a degree or two, and a few wispy clouds floated above us.

"Archie?" I said, threading some glittery ribbon through the middle of the scarves. "How do you know so much about school and how to fit in?"

Archer's hand hovered over Reggie's fur. "I've moved around a lot," he said. "Four schools in five years, actually."

"Really?" I said. "Were they all like Lockerton Primary?"

"Pretty much. They all have rules and homework and people that forget you as soon as you leave."

"I wouldn't forget you!" I said firmly. I was careful not to break eye contact so he knew I was as seriously serious as serious could be.

"I know," he said, his freckly forehead crinkling. "But you're not like the others."

Not like the others? What did that mean?

I had always been taught to celebrate our differences, but Mrs Spencer said my Backpack of Cheer didn't follow prontocall (whatever that meant),

Miss Eversley looked at my elfsolls like they might spontaneously combust, and Alice and Liena treated me like I was from another planet all together. Maybe I should try to be more like them? Maybe I should blend in like Archer did? Maybe I should talk a little less about Christmas and a little more about hairstyles and horse riding and dance club?

"You OK?" Archer said. "You've gone into some sort of trance."

"Dance club!" I snapped, jerking my head up. "I mean . . . Yes, all good."

Archer chuckled under his breath.

"So how come your family move around so much?" I said, concentrating on my next round of stitches to hide my embarrassment.

"Because I've had more than one family," Archer said matter-of-factly.

"More than one?" I said, letting the scarves fall into my lap. "What do you mean?"

Reggie nudged Archer's hand so he could tuck his

head even further into Archer's lap.

"Calling them my family is the easiest way to describe them," Archer explained. "But I suppose it's not that simple."

He took a moment to gather his thoughts and then spoke again. "When my birth parents weren't able to look after me, they found me another family who cared for me like I was one of their own," Archer explained. "That was the first time I moved."

"Does that mean you're adopted?"

"Sort of," Archer said, stroking Reggie's mane. "Adoption is when you find a permanent family to live with. I'm a foster kid, which means we stay with a family for a few months or years until we find our forever home."

"Sort of like how we're looking after the reindeer until the garden centre can take them?" I asked.

"I suppose so, yeah."

I'd never thought about the different types of families out there. I mean, I know we're lucky to be living on Sleigh Ride Avenue with a wrapping room and twenty-eight Christmas trees, but I never stopped to think that some people might not have a permanent home at all.

"Have you had lots of foster families then?" I said.

Archer's face fell into a thoughtful frown. His eyes wandered off as he stared into the distance, trapped in a memory. "A few," he said eventually. "But now I'm living with Pa at the children's home. There's a few of us there. Lennie and Rodge are older than me. They've been teaching me all the shortcuts and cheats on the PlayStation, and they eat so many packets of crisps, Pa says they'll probably turn into potatoes one day. Then there's Fran, Lennie's sister. She likes to boss us all around even though she's younger than us and she makes the best chocolate chip cookies – but don't tell her I told you that."

Archer's cheeks flushed red, but I put it down to the steamy evening air and the fact that he had a slightly overweight donkey draped across his lap.

"Why didn't you tell me earlier?" I said. "About

the children's home and living with P— hang on, do you all call him Pa?"

Archer smiled. "It's short for Patrick. Patrick Lenton. And he's a legend. Although his taste for music isn't great."

Archer seemed so calm and relaxed, not at all like the shy, nervous Archer I was used to. If anything, *I* was the one that felt weird about his revelation and I didn't even know why.

"I'm sorry I didn't tell you earlier," he added. "It's not the easiest thing to talk about. Plus, we've only been friends for two days."

Only two days? That was the longest friendship I'd ever had, unless you counted the elf friends from my hobby tree, but they only spoke to me in my dreams, so I guess that didn't count.

"I suppose it takes a bit longer to find out everything about a person?" I said eventually.

Archer laughed. "Not if your name's Holly Carroll. I've never met someone who talks as much as you do.

Are you going for a world record or something?"

I opened my mouth in pretend shock. "How dare you!" I gasped, chucking all my spare balls of wool at him. "There's nothing wrong with being inquisitive. Take that. And that."

"Inquisitive is one way to look at it!" Archer replied, batting the wool across the paddock for Reggie to catch. "Blimey. How are you so good at this?"

"I'm Lapland's reigning Junior Snowball Fight Champion," I said, pummelling the balls of wool at him with strength and precision and a fancy flick of the wrist. "You'll have to do more than that to beat me."

"A Snowball Fight *Champion*?" Archer cried. He struggled to keep up, ducking left and right like a tennis player trying to swipe the wool balls away. "How is that fair? I've only seen proper snow once and that was when I had tonsillitus and was stuck in bed for a week."

"I think it's called tinsil-itus," I corrected, scooping up a slobbery ball of wool that Reggie spat out at my feet. "And are you telling me that you've never experienced actual snow?"

"Only the kind that lasts about half an hour and turns to mush as soon as it hits the ground. Definitely not enough to have a proper snowball fight."

I dropped my last ball of wool and let my mouth hang open. "But snow signals new beginnings and fresh starts," I said. "There's a reason Father Christmas lives in Lapland where it snows all the time. Snow brings miracles, and so does he."

Archer stared at me like I was speaking another language.

"Have you never felt the magic of a snowdrop?" I said. "Or the power of a snowstorm? Have you never felt like your life was being refreshed?"

"Like my life was being refreshed?" Archer laughed. "Where do you come up with this stuff?"

"I just mean. . . new beginnings. . . fresh starts. . . no?"

Archer shook his head. Oh.

THE SNOW-STORM

24

I woke up the next morning full of baubles. I'd stayed awake the whole night (or maybe it was twenty minutes), thinking about how much Archer had opened up to me. It felt good getting to know someone inside out. It was like he was becoming a member of the family, and I didn't realise friendship could feel like that.

In fact, the thought of having not one, not two, but three best friends by the end of the day filled me with so much joy, I thought I might wet myself in nercitement (nervous excitement). So I hop-skipped through the school gates and into the playground where Alice and Liena were surrounded by a group of squealing students, fussing teachers and nattering parents with giant pushchairs.

"Sign up for the September Soirée committee," Alice shouted from the middle of the crowd. She was handing a clipboard around and proudly displaying her class rep badge.

"And don't forget to sponsor our danceathon!" Liena added, waving a giant banner above her head with a photo of her and Alice on it. Mrs Spencer was even asking them to pose for photos for the school newsletter.

I could feel my tummy gurgle with jealger. You know what I mean, don't you – when you're not sure if you're jealous or just hungry? They were getting so much attention, spreading so much cheer, doing so much good for the community, and I *had* to be a part of it.

I'd been preparing myself all morning. I'd wrapped their friendship scarves inside glittery cardboard tubes and written letters that listed all the reasons I wanted to be their friend (because they were good at spreading cheer, they liked to impress Miss Eversley, and because Alice's spiky ears were the stuff elf-dreams were made of). I'd even baked them a fresh batch of mince pies, which admittedly were slightly crushed and now half-eaten inside my pockets.

This was it. My moment to shine. I opened my mouth to start singing my Lockerton Primary Christmas carol – and that was when I saw him.

Archer was circling the crowd, his lip curled and his head down, slipping by unnoticed as usual. Unnoticed by everyone, that is, but me. Even from a distance I could tell he had angry eyes and flushed cheeks. Maybe he'd even been crying?

Something wasn't adding up. I'd seen Archer confused and curious. I'd seen him happy and content and bemused and unsure. But this was an Archer I'd never seen. Never in my three whole days of knowing him.

"Archie!" I yelled, waving my hands above my head and almost knocking myself out with the friendship scarf tubes. I ran towards him, occasionally glancing at Alice and Liena and the bustling crowd around them.

"Archie," I panted, reaching him as the bell rang and tapping him on the shoulder. "Are you OK? What's wrong? Shall I sing you a —"

"They think they're so clever," Archer spat, glaring at Alice and

Liena as they packed up their posters and posed for one last photo for Mrs Spencer. "They have no idea how to put others first or help the community. They don't even care about improving the school unless it benefits them."

"You're annoyed about Alice and Liena?" I said, my thoughts more jumbled than the tangled fairy lights hiding inside my Hollyhood. "But I thought you didn't want to be a class rep?"

"I don't. And I don't know why you want to be one either. There are more important things in the world than painting the school red or singing carols at lunchtime."

"But spreading cheer –"

Archer rolled his eyes. "Helps make the world a better place. Yeah. You've said."

"I don't understand what's going on," I said. "Last night you were happy to help me make friendship scarves for Alice and Liena and now –"

"The scarves are a waste of time," Archer snapped.

"Open your eyes, Holly. Christmas can't cure everything."

He stormed away past the Year Five block, round the back of the toilets and through the double doors towards the office. With his long hair covering his eyes and his hands clenched, it was like there was a snowstorm building inside him, one that even *he* couldn't see out of.

I tried to move my feet but they were glued to the ground. My hands were shaking.

What in Santa's sleigh was going on?

A DIFFERENT KIND OF CHRISTMAS

25

Did you know you can learn things about people without even speaking to them? It's true. Today I learnt that Archer is *great* at playing hide and seek. He wasn't at registration or Maths class, he appeared for two seconds in Drama and then left again, he was nowhere to be seen at lunch time, and during our afternoon science experiment, he was paired with Daniel and Marie because they wanted to create some kind of skateboarding gravity test and they were the only ones that knew how to skateboard. I was on the opposite side of the classroom, monitoring the affects of gravity and air-resistance on my miniature sleigh replica, but even that couldn't stop me from gazing across the room every few minutes.

At least Archer looked like he was back to his quiet, nervous self. He was only speaking when Daniel or Marie asked him a question, and he seemed more concerned with a spot on the wall than returning my enthusiastic waves across the classroom. In fact, it wasn't until after the bell rang at 3:15 that I said more than two words to him at all.

"Archer!" I called, waving him down at the school gate. "I hope you've had a Thrilling Thursday?"

With not so much as a grunt, Archer walked straight past me, his gaze fixed on the ground.

What could I have possibly done? Had I forgotten to invent a best friends handshake? Was he annoyed I hadn't knitted him a friendship scarf yet?

I ran over the different scenarios in my head. Maybe he was just having one of those 'down days'

I'd heard about. I wondered how to make it up to him. Being cheerful was contagious, so maybe I just had to pass it on?

"Archer!" I called again, running alongside him. "I said –"

"Not now, Holly. I need to get home."

"Maybe I can come with you?" I said, shooting him a grin so toothy I could've been mistaken for Reggie's twin. "We can make those Holarwiches we planned. Or we can write a new Christmas carol? Or you can come to mine and play with Reggie? I know he'd love to see you."

"I don't have time for any of that."

"So why don't we –"

"Look," Archer said, stopping so suddenly, someone accidentally rammed a pushchair into his ankles. "Maybe we shouldn't be friends. I've had fun and everything, but let's face it. We're not exactly compatible."

"We're more than compatible – we're

comsplatable!" I said, thinking that was the perfect word for snowball fighting best friends.

A corner of his mouth crinkled. "You're funny, Hols. Really funny. But you care about knitting scarves and stuffing snowman cushions. I have other things to worry about. Important things."

"Then why don't I help you?" I suggested. "Spreading cheer is all about –"

"You don't get it, do you?" Archer yelled, his cheeks turning red.

I stumbled back.

"Have you never stopped to think about people that are too ill to celebrate Christmas? Or those that are homeless and have nowhere to go on Christmas day? Or even those that don't have any friends or family to spend it with?" He was breathing hard, his chest rising and falling with every word he spoke. "I don't want to get angry, Holly, but you need to open your eyes. We don't all live in that perfect world of yours."

A blizzard of thoughts whirred in my head. "But –"

"There's nothing else to say," he said, lowering his voice. "Enjoy your eve— I mean, have a Thrilling Thursday. I'll see you around." He strode across the zebra crossing, turned down a narrow lane, and disappeared out of sight.

I stood, blinking at the empty street corner, my heart crushed like a mound of trampled snow. Was it really that easy to lose a best friend? Like dropping a glass bauble and watching it smash into a thousand pieces? Could something like that be repaired?

"Holly!" a voice squealed behind me. "What was that about?"

I wiped the tears from my eyes and turned around. "Alice," I whimpered, standing a little taller to mirror her perfect posture. "Liena. I've been trying to find you all day."

"We've been busy," Liena said, tossing her hair off her shoulder to reveal her shiny class rep badge. "Mrs Spencer invited us to an exclusive class rep meeting to discuss our plans for the school. She was *really* impressed. We might be the best class reps she's ever had!"

I forced a smile and tried to steady my voice. "That's great," I said, chucking my backpack on the ground and hoping the friendship scarves weren't too squashed inside. "I –"

"Ho, ho, ho!" Dad's voice boomed from the speaker inside the bag. "Merry Christmas one and all!"

Alice smirked and Liena's forehead wrinkled. They were giving me that look again. The 'Christmas is really lame and so are you for celebrating it all year round' kind of look. Maybe Archer was right. Maybe you *were* only supposed to celebrate Christmas once a year. Is that why he didn't want to be my friend?

"So you're *really* into Christmas?" Alice said, hiding her grin behind her hand.

I shrugged. Was this some kind of friendship test? And if so, what was I meant to say?

"I've never really taken part in the whole Christmas thing," Liena added before I could answer.

"But we do celebrate the Chinese New Year. We still eat food together and spend time with family, but we have fireworks and firecrackers, and instead of gifts, we give red envelopes with money inside."

Fireworks, firecrackers and red envelopes? That sounded cheertastic! What else didn't I know about the Chinese New Year? My face must've been doing something really funky because Alice and Liena took a step back as if I might be sick all over their shiny black shoes.

"You're not going to cry, are you?" Alice said. "Yeah. You do know that not everyone celebrates Christmas, right?"

"Of course," I said, my heart stamping faster than reindeer hooves on an icy roof. " I'm not *that* into Christmas. Like, it's not an obsession or anything. We don't have reindeer or a wrapping room or an ice-skating rink or anything like that."

Liena laughed. "Right. Because that would be ridiculous!"

I nodded shyly as Alice's gaze fell upon the Backpack of Cheer.

"That's just an old bag I found," I added hastily. "I'm getting a new one at the weekend. And the elfsolls and class rep speech were just, ummm . . ."

"A dare?" Liena suggested.

"Yes! Exactly. A dare that got a bit out of control."

"I'll say," said Alice.

"Anyway, I'm putting all that Christmas stuff behind me now . . ." I paused as the words caught in my throat. "And I'd really like to be your class rep. I mean, I'd like to help with your friend. I mean . . ."

My mind went back and forth as I tried to decide whether to give them their scarves or not. Here I was, on the verge of making two new friends, but all I could think about was the one I just lost. What would Archer do? He wouldn't sing a carol, that was for sure. He wouldn't ask them what they wanted for Christmas. And he certainly wouldn't mention the squashed mince pies in his pocket.

"I'd really like to help out at your dance club," I said eventually. "And maybe I could hand some leaflets out for your September Soirée?"

Alice and Liena looked at each other with smiling eyes.

"I guess we could do with an extra pair of hands," Alice said, guiding me towards Mrs Spencer's office where they'd left all of their plans and projection charts.

"Yeah, I'm sure we can find a supportive role for you somewhere," Liena agreed.

They muttered something about my great craft skills and big ideas and how I could be an art set (or was it 'asset'?) to the team, and then they spent the next hour trying to decide what shade of purple to make the soirée invitations. It wasn't until Mrs Spencer shooed us out at five o'clock that I realised I'd spent the whole time biting my tongue, avoiding the words 'Christmas' and 'cheer', and worrying about Archer. In fact, the only thing I managed to contribute was the suggestion of a red carpet (so at least there would be *some* festiveness at the soirée) and a three-tier chocolate fountain (although they didn't seem too fond of changing the chocolate to gravy for some reason).

I wondered if this was what friendship was supposed to be like. Maybe you're meant to change yourself to fit in with the crowd. Maybe you're supposed to hide your passions and interests if they're not the same as everyone else's. Maybe you should say and do whatever you can just to feel accepted?

Alice stepped forward to give me a hug as the caretaker locked the school gate behind us.

"This has been—"

"THRILLING THURSDAY, EVERYONE!" a deep voice boomed

from across the street.

"DON'T FORGET TO SPREAD CHEER WHEREVER YOU GO!"

Alice and Liena's heads shot up. No. Nope. No way. This wasn't happening. Not now.

Our Christmas car playlist belted out into the street as Dad's head appeared out of the window a few

feet away.

"YOU'RE MEANT TO SAY, 'LET'S SPREAD CHEER WITH A HO HO HO!'" he shouted. He waved his arms so gleefully, he knocked the car horn, which proceeded to play an entire verse of *Jingle Bells*. He couldn't have looked more delighted as he shoved his favourite green elf hat on top of his head and swayed from side to side, singing along to the sound of the horn.

I cringed. Where was Santa and his sleigh when you needed a quick getaway?

"That's not your *dad*, is it?" Alice gasped.

"No!" I laughed, making myself as small as possible and darting behind a nearby tree. "No, no. I've never seen that man in my life."

ZERO

B y the time Dad had reeled off all the cheer he'd spread that day, I arrived home with an ache in my chest and my head feeling like a shaken snow globe. Mum said I was probably tired from all the cheer spreading and told me to take some down time in the wrapping room with a mince pie or two, but what exactly was that supposed to achieve? Archer was right. Spreading cheer wasn't always the answer to everything. In fact, the more I thought about it, the stupider I felt for trying to ram Christmas down everyone's throat.

I mean, think of all the different people that can't

celebrate Christmas. Wrapping presents wouldn't help the homeless. Adding glitter and a bow wouldn't reunite someone with their family. Boxing the perfectly symmetrical gift wouldn't cure someone of an illness. And that's not even taking other cultures or religions into consideration, like Liena and her Chinese New Year. Had I been living my entire life stuffed inside a stocking?

"Hollypops!" Mum called. "Time for dinner."

I switched the festadio and tree lights off and trudged down the stairs.

"It's your favourite," Mum said, straightening my Christmas cracker and pulling my chair out for me. "Turkey dinner with all the trimmings."

I glanced around the kitchen like I was seeing it for the first time. Every inch of space was filled with snowflake counter-tops, snowball door handles and tinsel wrapped round every appliance. There were lights attached to the ceiling, red bows on the backs of our chairs, and the table was covered in a miniature scene of Lapland.

"We've been thinking about this year's hobby tree," Dad said, already helping himself to extra sprouts. "Would you still like a knitting tree, Hols? How are the decorations coming along?"

I stared at my plate. It was overflowing with so much food, we had to put the parsnips and Yorkshire puddings in bowls at the side.

"Actually, Dad, I think I'd like a lost tree this year," I murmured, sliding into my chair.

Mum and Dad paused, their forks halfway to their mouths.

"A lost tree?" Dad repeated. "A hobby tree that's *lost*?"

I shrugged. "Why not?"

Mum and Dad looked at each other with crinkled eyebrows.

"That sounds mighty inventive, Hols," Dad said eventually. "Why don't we put our heads together later and see what we can come up with?"

I rolled my eyes. Trust Dad to take my idea literally. I bet he'd come up with the most over-the-top 'lost' tree he could think of, when all I really meant was that I didn't want one at all.

I pushed the food around my plate and tried to block out the carols playing on the festadio. Nothing felt right any more. Not now I knew how weird it was to celebrate Christmas all year. Not when I'd had to lie just to make a friend or two. Not when I knew there were problems in the world that couldn't be cured with a handwritten note or perfectly timed Christmas song.

"So!" Dad clapped with his Cheshire cat grin. "Shall we share our cheerometer ratings for the day?"

Great.

"I'll go, I'll go!" Mum squealed, smoothing her apron down. "My cheerometer rating is a ten, obviously. I designed a new limited edition reindeer apron, complete with detachable antlers, inspired by Reggie. Then I made a fruit cake for Mrs Appleton across the road – her daughters are coming to visit her this weekend and she can't leave the house in this heat, so I offered to help. I even made a new contact in Italy who wants to put an order in for some aprons, so it's been a rather wonderful day all round."

"Bravo!" Dad cried, pecking Mum on the cheek. "I'd give my day a ten, too. I persuaded my boss to decorate the garden centre for Christmas next month, he's put me in charge of designing Santa's grotto, and I met someone from the council who said I could help with the Lockerton Christmas Parade."

Ivy clapped her hands and managed to lob half of her mashed potato across the table and straight into my hair.

"Even Ivykins has had a ten out of ten day, haven't you, my angel?" Mum cooed. "She made some Christmas-tree finger paintings for the post office and she learned how to say 'bauble'. Didn't you, my clever girl? Yes you did! Yes you did!"

Dad ruffled Ivy's hair. "And what about you, Hols?" he said, eyeing up the turkey on my plate. "What's

your cheerometer rating for the day?"

What was I supposed to say? That I had a big argument with Archer and lost my best friend? That I lied to Alice and Liena just so they would like me? That I was having second thoughts about the whole point of Christmas?

"Holly," Mum said, her voice going all high-pitched. "You know it's rude to ignore someone

when they're speaking to you."

"And why haven't you eaten any of your dinner yet?" Dad said. "You've barely said two words since you got in. I know you weren't yourself on the way home, but –"

"It's zero!" I shouted, pushing my plate away. "My cheerometer rating is zero. Is that what you wanted to hear?"

"Hollypops, I —"

I threw my hands in the air and pushed my chair back. "Do you even realise how embarrassing this all is?"

"Embarrassing? Snowflake, I don't —"

"You do know that nobody else celebrates Christmas every day, don't you?"

"Well, I —"

"It's just us," I shouted. "It's weird and it's over the top and totally unnecessary. It just looks like we're showing off all the time. We try to make out that we're good and kind and cheerful, but we can't be that good and kind if we don't stop to think about all the people that don't even get a Christmas. All we think about is making ourselves look good."

"I'm not sure that's the—"

"Do you even know what it feels like to have everyone laugh at you?" I sobbed. "Or what it's like to constantly say the wrong thing, or wear the wrong clothes or have everyone think you're strange?

Because that's what people think, you know. They think we're weird. I bet we've not had a single reply to our house warming party, have we?"

"Well, no, but –"

"And has anyone wished you a Merry Christmas since we've arrived?"

"The postman nearly –"

"And do you know that Mr Bleurgh is petitioning to remove us from the street?"

Mum and Dad stared at me. Ivy stopped playing with her food. The festadio faded to a crackle.

"Nobody wants us here," I said quietly. "Nobody wants to celebrate Christmas all year round." I gulped. "And I don't think I do either."

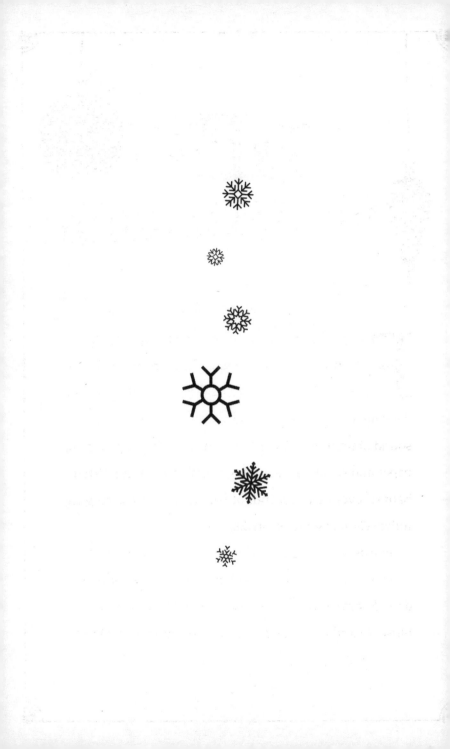

DE-CHRISTMAFIED

For the first time in forever, I went to bed in silence. The fire wasn't crackling in the living room, Mum and Dad weren't practising carols on the lawn or dancing to the festadio in the kitchen, I couldn't hear the sound of jingling bells or the distant tearing of wrapping paper and sticky tape, and Ivy wasn't screaming 'Where Santa?' every two seconds at bedtime. Even the singing toilet seat had gone on strike.

Is this what bedtime was supposed to feel like?

It was strange not to feel excited for the following day. Everything felt so uncertain, like when you blow a candle out and you're thrown into darkness.

Normally we had a routine with Christmas chores and inventions to make and cheer to spread, but tomorrow . . . tomorrow there would be none of that. In fact, I was determined to make tomorrow the first normal day of my new normal life where I'd make normal friends and do normal things.

Don't give me that look! How hard could being normal be?

❄

I stayed in my room all morning, trying to make myself look as unchristmassy as possible. I'd searched high and low for a plain black backpack like Archer's and a tinsel-less headband like Alice's, but all I could find was a plastic sandwich bag to carry my pencils, and an elastic band for my hair, which I knew I'd one hundred percent regret once it got caught in my curls.

By the time I walked out of the house, I felt ordinary, plain, *invisible*. This was it. My first average day for an average person in an average world where it wasn't Christmas every day.

"You there!" a voice bellowed, making me jump. "Come here at once."

Mr Bleurgh hobbled across the road with a clipboard in one hand and something big and hairy waddling behind him. "I assume this beast is yours?"

"Reggie!" I gasped. "Where have you been?"

"This monster was chewing my petunias and relieving himself on my award-winning grass," grumbled Mr Bleurgh. "Do you people go out of your way to make my life a misery?"

"I'm so sorry, Mr Bleurgh," I said. "Reggie didn't know what he was doing. He probably just wanted to say hello. Or compliment you on your pelunas."

"PETUNIAS," the old man snapped. "And he *absolutely* knew what he was doing. He was grinning at me through the window like a crazed clown. He should be locked up."

I gulped. "Locked up?"

"Much like children really," said Mr Bleurgh. "It wasn't like this in my day. All these bright lights and childish toys . . ." He motioned toward the hobby trees and snow maze. "Nowadays parents live through their children. They bend over backwards to make their offspring happy. I bet your parents don't really enjoy this, do they? I bet they do it all for you –"

"Holly?" Dad called, pulling the front door shut behind him. "Is everything OK?"

My eyes nearly fell from their sockets. "Dad! Is . . . is that you?"

He was wearing faded jeans and a plain black polo shirt with the garden centre logo on his chest. There was no Santa hat, no tinsel tool belt, no sparkle in his shoes or twinkle in his eyes.

"Reginald?" he said, striding across the lawn with a frown. "What have you been doing?"

"What *hasn't* he been doing!" Mr Bleurgh growled, handing Dad Reggie's deflated antlers. "This donkey is a –"

Dad and I gasped.

Mr Bleurgh's forehead wrinkled.

Reggie let out a sad whine.

"He's a *reindeer*," I said, taking Reggie from Mr Bleurgh and wrapping my arms around Reggie's neck. "The greatest reindeer in all the land."

"And you are deluded," scoffed Mr Bleurgh. "This is a donkey. Your house is an abomination. And your family are –"

"Aware that we may have caused some upset," Dad interrupted. He looked smaller somehow, less Dad-like. It was like looking at a stranger. "Holly brought some issues to our attention last night," he said with weary eyes. "And we understand we may have caused some offence with our decorations. We'll be de-christmafying the house shortly."

"We will?" I said.

Dad nodded. "And ourselves. The last thing we want to do is upset our neighbours or friends. Or anyone in our own family, for that matter." He looked at me so intensely, I wanted to cry.

"I see," Mr Bleurgh huffed, glancing at his

clipboard. "So this little blighter won't be ruining any more gardens, your house will be restored to its former glory, and you won't be hosting your little welcome party?"

"We'll do whatever makes our Holly happy," Dad said. He forced a smile and then led Reggie back to the stables.

I couldn't think straight. Reggie was in trouble. The decorations were coming down. Dad had lost his sparkle. Mr Bleurgh was *smiling*? This was supposed to be the first normal day of my life – but things didn't feel normal at all.

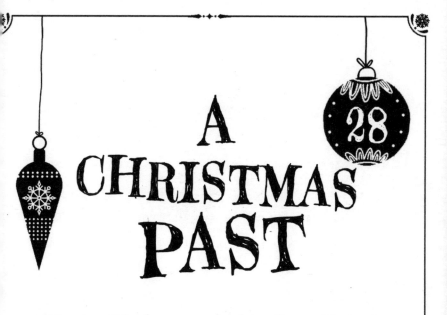

A CHRISTMAS PAST

We drove to school in silence. No jingle bell car horn, no Christmas carol singalong, no wishing everyone a joyous day out of the window. Dad was so quiet, I had to check more than once that he hadn't fallen asleep.

"Dad?" I said eventually. "Can I ask you something?"

"Of course," he said, trying a bit too hard to keep his voice light and cheery. "What's troubling you?"

"I've been wondering *why* we love Christmas so much," I said. "Is there an actual reason, or do you just do it because you think it makes me happy?"

It was a question that had kept me up all night. Were we just born with extra cheer? Were we distant relatives of Father Christmas so Christmas spirit was in our blood? Or perhaps there was a Christmas miracle that bestowed us with extra amounts of joy?

"Well . . ." Dad said, shuffling in his seat. ""You know that Christmas feeling we get all year round?"

I nodded.

"Have you ever thought that some people might feel the very opposite of that? No magic in the air. No anticipation in their bellies. No utter elation when someone wishes them a merry day?"

"That's what I was talking about last night," I said. "*We're* the odd ones out. I don't think we're supposed to feel like that all the time."

"It's funny you should say that," Dad said, raising his eyebrows. "Because your mum–"

I glanced at Dad out of the corner of my eye. "What about Mum?"

"Let's just say, there wasn't a lot of magic in her

world when she was your age. She was lucky to get twenty-four hours of joy on Christmas day, in fact."

I whirled around so fast I dislodged a forgotten cinnamon stick from my Hollyhood and sent it flying out of the window. "WHAT?" I gasped.

"It was a long time ago," said Dad. "Back when she lived with her parents."

It was strange to think that Mum had a life before me. A life before our family home and trips to Lapland. A life where Christmas *wasn't* celebrated every day? "Your granny and grandad had an . . . *unusual* relationship," Dad said, turning into the high street. "They loved each other very much, but they loved arguing more."

I pulled a face that was a cross between smelling a really bad fart and falling out of bed. "How can someone love arguing?"

Dad shrugged. "Beats me. But they did. They argued about everything. They fought over who should make the toast in the morning and then disagreed over how dark or light the toast should be. Granny wanted hers so burnt it looked like a piece of coal, and Grandad said anything more than 'warm bread' was unacceptable. They'd spend so long arguing over the size and colour and what sort of plate to put it on that they'd let the toast go cold and end up throwing it away."

"They sound a bit strange," I said.

"The only time they didn't argue was at Christmas," Dad went on. "For those special few hours every year, Granny and Grandad went out of each other's way to make each other smile. Grandad burnt Granny's toast and cut it into a Christmas tree shape. Granny let Grandad watch whatever he wanted on TV. They even slow-danced in the kitchen while they washed the dishes, even though Granny hated dancing and Grandad would do anything to avoid going near soap and water."

"So that's why Mum loves Christmas?" I said. "Because it was the one day a year her parents didn't argue?"

"Yes. And so she tried to replicate the joy they felt for Christmas throughout the year. On the twenty-fifth of June ..."

"Half-Christmas?"

"That's right. On the twenty-fifth of June, your mum would ask her parents to put a tree and decorations up, and she'd try to recreate the magic of Christmas morning. Christmas was the one thing they agreed on, and your mum did everything she could to spread that across the year."

I checked that I understood what Dad was saying. "Celebrating Christmas made her parents happy, so she tried to make them happy every day?"

"Exactly."

"But what about all the people that don't like Christmas?" I said quietly. "Making her parents happy is one thing, but what if our celebrations actually upset some people or cause offence? What if some people hate Christmas so much we're actually doing the opposite of spreading cheer?"

Dad thought for a moment. "Well, yes, we wouldn't want that, would we? But why the change of heart, Snowflake? We thought you loved Christmas as much as us?

"I do . . ." I gulped. "I mean, I *did*."

"But not any more?"

I took a deep breath. "I'm the weird Christmas girl that tries to make everything about spreading cheer," I explained gloomily. "Nobody wants to be around me. They think I'm strange. *I* think I'm strange."

"Being strange is not a bad thing, Snowflake," said Dad. "It means you're unique. It means you're human."

"Maybe I don't want to be unique. Maybe I –"

"Hey, isn't that your friend Archer?" Dad said.

I wound the window down and frantically searched the tree-lined road. "Where?" I cried.

"See that house with the 'For Sale' sign?" Dad said. "Beside the children's home?"

I flung myself across Dad's lap to get a better look, accidentally setting off the *Jingle Bells* car horn. Everyone turned to look at us – dog-walkers, a man in a wheelchair, a group of children crossing the road ... and Archer, whose red cheeks and puffy eyes could be seen from halfway down the street.

"I think you might need to spread some Christmas cheer today after all, Hols," said Dad as we sped on down the road.

I swallowed a lump in my throat. I wasn't so sure. Archer had said how Christmas couldn't cure everything.

And something in the back of my mind told me I was about to find out why.

THE SIGN

29

After a brief catch-up with Alice and Liena about song lists and table plans for the September Soirée, I spied Archer lurking around our lunch spot. His hands were in his pockets and his head was down, and despite every voice in my head telling me to leave him alone and give him some space, I found myself using my best secret Santa moves to get to him as quickly as possible.

"Hols?" he said, seeing right through my tip-toeing and tree hiding and shimmying-down-the-chimney routine. "Can I have a word?"

"Oh," I said, scratching my head. "You *want* to speak to me?"

"I need to apologise," he said, acting like a lost little lamb again. "Will you hear me out?"

A flood of emotion surged through me. What was I supposed to do? Forget everything he'd said about not being friends? Thank him for helping me realise how weird my family were? Push out a cheeky fart to break the ice?

"I'm new to this friends thing," I blurted out before Archer could say anything else. "I let Christmas take over and that was wrong. I should've known that you'd have your own interests and hobbies, and that celebrating Christmas all year isn't for everyone. I shouldn't have pushed you into doing the class rep speech either. And I'm sorry I kept asking to swap snow – I mean, *sand*wiches – they were just so delicious and I didn't know when –"

"You've done nothing wrong," Archer said eventually.

I paused. "Oh . . . then why didn't you want to be my friend?"

Archer breathed out slowly and made himself comfortable on the ground. "Two nights ago, after I got home from helping you with the friendship scarves, I had a phone call from some friends I made at an old foster home."

I titled my head to one side and joined him on the concrete. Where was this going?

"We'd planned to meet up next weekend and go to the skate park," Archer went on. "We do that sometimes, just to catch up and hang out. Before I moved in with Pa, we hung out a lot. Our old foster carer said we'd live in each other's pockets if we could."

I smiled, imagining what it would be like to spend weekends hanging out with friends instead of present wrapping, ice-skating and carol singing.

"It sounds like you were really close," I said.

Archer nodded. "They're like my family. Eli's the oldest. He's twelve, but nearly thirteen, and he's crazy good with numbers. You can give him any sum and he'll do it quicker than a calculator. Then there's Carson, who's our age, and their little brother, William, but we call him 'Wreck It Will' because he basically destroys everything in his path."

"They sound great," I said, wondering if it was too early to ask to meet them.

"Turns out, they're moving," Archer said, his voice wobbling in the middle. "To a new foster home up north and. . ."

"And?"

Archer took a deep breath. "I might never see them again."

"But you said they're like your family!" I cried. "Isn't there something you can do?"

Archer shook his head. "Foster kids don't have a say in where we end up. The homes are always nice and we're looked after well, but we get attached to each other and so splitting up is . . ." Archer looked away, his eyes locked on the ground. ". . . Hard."

I tried to imagine what that would be like, but the only thing I could compare it to was Mr Bleurgh trying to evict us from Sleigh Ride Avenue. And as awful as that would've been, at least we had each other. Archer's friends were moving house, they'd be far away from Archer who was basically like a brother to them. How was that fair?

"So you were upset because you might not get to see Eli, Carson and Will again?" I said.

"I was upset for a lot of reasons," Archer said, playing with his hands nervously. "There I was, talking about grottos and presents and making holarwiches with you. I live in an amazing home with Pa. I've been spending my evenings playing with reindeer – and my friends don't even know where they're going to be for Christmas. It's just not right. And then all Alice and Liena could talk about was their stupid dance club and September Soirée, and it riled me up."

"But why didn't you just tell me this before?" I said. "I would've understood."

"I know," Archer said. "But you also would've tried to help by spreading Christmas magic or whatever, and I just didn't see the point. There's nothing we can do."

I could feel my brain whirring and fizzing, trying to find a solution. It couldn't help itself. It was programmed to spread cheer and fix problems, and I couldn't turn it off if I tried.

"What if there *is* something we could do?" I said.

"Like what?"

"What if Pa invited them to stay with you?" I suggested. "Then you could all live together."

"Pa's place only has four bedrooms," Archer said. "And they're all taken."

I tried again. "Well, what if we had them stay with us at Sleigh Ride Avenue? Just until they found somewhere permanent?"

"There are rules with fostering, Holly," said Archer. "You can't just click your fingers and make it happen. Unless you've got a Christmas miracle in your back pocket, I've just got to face the fact that I won't see them for a while."

For what was probably the first time in my life, I let my mind go silent. It needed time to think, to imagine, to contemflate. "Archie?" I said eventually. "Did you mean it when you said you didn't want to be my friend any more?"

"Of course not," Archer said, resting his head in his hands. "I was just angry. I haven't put much effort into making friends at school. I never saw the point. Every other time I've made friends, I've had to leave them behind, so it was simpler not to make any in the first place. Until you came along."

"And what was different about me?" I said.

Archer grinned. "You didn't really give me a choice."

I cringed. I guess I had come on a bit strong. All those times I forced Archer to come to my house, to eat lunch with me or to keep me company as I knitted friendship scarves. I never even asked if he wanted to!

"I'm sorry," I said. "I'd just wanted a friend for so,

so long. A proper friend."

"Me too," Archer said. "I mean, I've got friends from the other children's homes and stuff, but being friends with someone at school is different. It's a choice."

"So you're not mad that I wanted to spend so much time with you?" I asked nervously.

Archer shook his head. "I suppose it's a sign of a good friendship? A sign that–"

"SIGN!" I shouted.

Archer jumped. "Er, what?"

"THE SIGN!" I said again.

Archer's forehead crumpled.

"The sign, Archer! The 'For Sale' sign beside the children's home." Ideas exploded in my head like fireworks. "There's a house up for sale beside the children's home, isn't there? I saw it when we drove past on the way to school."

"I think so. Why?"

"What if Pa *bought* the house?" I shouted. "What if he extended the children's home so there weren't just four rooms, and then Eli and Carson and Will could all live with you?"

"It's not that easy," Archer said. "Pa doesn't have the money or the time or the –"

"But what if he DID have the money?"

"He *doesn't*, Holly!" Archer said. "And Christmas cheer won't make him a millionaire!"

"You're not listening to me," I said, jumping to my feet. "What if we could *give* him the money? What if we could use the September Soirée to raise the funds he needs to buy the house? What if he had the support of the whole village?"

Archer snorted. "Impossible."

"Nothing is impossible," I said, catching Alice and Liena's eye across the playground. "Not when it comes to spreading cheer."

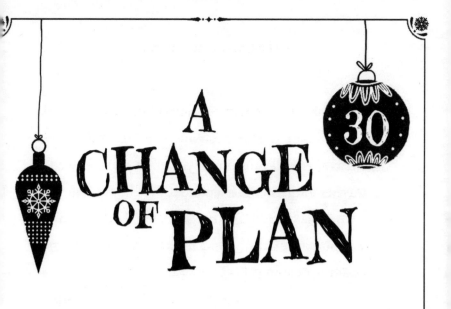

A CHANGE OF PLAN

30

"Turn the fairy lights off, Mum. I'll put the festadio in the cupboard. Do we have time to remove the ribbons from the ceiling?" I ran around the wrapping room like a wounded wind-up toy without an off button. I crashed into the Christmas tree, accidentally yanked some rolls of wrapping paper off the walls, and almost knocked the doors off the stationery cupboard.

"What's wrong, Snowdrop?" Mum said, whimpering as she flicked the switch on the Christmas tree lights.

"Nothing," I groaned, wondering if I had time to

hoover the glitter off the carpet. "We just need to hurry up. They'll be here soon."

I had spent all morning trying to convince Archer that we could help his friends. At first he thought the heatwave had gotten to me and that I needed a lie down, but once Alice and Liena agreed that raising money for the children's home would be the greatest and most important fundraiser in Lockerton Primary history, he gradually came round. We then spent most of the lunch break speaking to Mrs Spencer about the change of plan, calling Pa to check he was on board, and sharing our ~~snowiches~~ sandwiches amongst each other. It was probably one of the greatest lunches of my life, and there wasn't a single Christmas card, cracker or Santa napkin in sight.

But then, of course, I had to go and ruin it all. I couldn't help myself! I was too excited.

What did you do? I hear you ask?

I invited Archer, Alice and Liena to my house to finish planning the fundraiser. Yes, to my over-the-top Christmas house. To my over-the-top Christmas house with an ice-rink, pet reindeer, ice sculptures in the hallway and a billion other things I said I didn't have.

I know, I know. I have zero elf control.

"Here we are," Dad sung, guiding Alice and Liena into the wrapping room. "Would you girls like some festive gro . . ."

I coughed and sent Dad my harshest 'please shut up' stare.

"Oh, er, never mind," he grinned nervously. He was wearing his plain black polo shirt from earlier and looked two feet smaller without a Santa hat on his head. "I'll leave you to it, Snowflaaa . . ."

I shook my head.

"I mean . . . You know where I am if you need me," he croaked.

Mum fussed with her non-glittery hair and slid a plate of snacks onto the table. "Here are some RICE cakes for you all," she said, glancing at me to check she'd said the right thing. "And as you can see, they're on a plain white plate. There's no extra christmasness here."

"And just ignore the decorations," Dad added. "We're storing them for later in the year, isn't that right, Hols?"

I nodded as Dad let out a sigh of relief and edged toward the door.

"Well then, if there's anything we can do, just let us . . ."

"Sorry I'm late," Archer called, appearing in the doorway slightly out of breath. "Pa was– oh." He looked into all four corners of the room. "Where have the Christmas aprons gone? And the bow boxes? Are those ice cakes? Where's the music from the festadio?"

Alice and Liena looked at each other with confused expressions.

"What are you on about?" I said, laughing a little too loudly. "Let's just, er, get on with organising the fundraiser, shall we? Where shall we start? Who wants to go first?"

Mum and Dad edged into the corridor without so much as a 'ho-ho-ho' or festive jig and I guided Alice and Liena to a corner of the room that had as few decorations as possible. They spent the next ten minutes gawping at the wrapping paper walls as Archer waved to Reggie outside the window and I tried to act like having a wrapping room and diva donkey was as normal as a singing toilet seat.

"So," Alice said, grabbing an ice cake off the plate. "How are we going to raise enough money for an entire house? They're not exactly cheap, are they?"

"Didn't Pa say something about a de-poo-sit?" I said, sitting opposite Alice on the carpet. "Where he only needs *some* of the money?"

"I think it's called a deposit," Archer replied, grinning at my latest made-up word. "And yeah . . . he's speaking to his bank manager about it tomorrow. I've also spoken to my social worker and she's going to help us apply for funding from a charity, which I guess could . . ."

"Social worker?" I said, screwing my face up in confusion. "What's a social worker?"

"They're people that check in on us, ask us how we're doing, see if we're happy," Archer shrugged. "Lots of us have social workers at the children's home."

"And their job is to help you with things?"

"Basically, yeah. I've had a few sessions this week. Like when Mrs Terse pulled me out of registration and then when I was late for the class rep speech and–"

"So that's where you were!" I cried, kicking myself for not asking him sooner. Apparently I had been so stuck in my own Christmassy world that I failed to find out where he kept disappearing to. Some best friend I was.

"I think you'd be pretty good as a social worker," Archer said seriously. "They're sort of like professional cheer spreaders."

My heart jolted. "A professional cheer-spreader? Is that a real thing?"

"When you're not being a fashion designer for

Mrs Claus, a Christmas parade organiser in New York and a shop owner so you can sell all your festive inventions, obviously!" I smiled widely. Archer had really been paying attention.

"That sounds like my dream j–" I caught myself just in time. "I mean, oh no, I . . . umm."

Alice and Liena looked at me with raised eyebrows. "Holly, are you–"

"Fine," I smiled, frantically offering them another ice cake. "Absolutely fine. Let's figure out how we can raise more money, yeah? What if we make the invitations ourselves? What if everyone brings some food so we don't need to pay for caterers? What if we have a raffle?"

After a few moments of awkward silence, Alice and Liena started scribbling notes on their projection charts, oblivious to the strange glances Archer was sending my way, like he was about to expose me for the giant fraud that I am.

I took a deep breath and tried to calm my nerves. This is what being normal feels like, right?

THIS CAN'T BE HAPPENING

31

Two weeks later, we arrived at school with boxes of balloons, signs for the car park and some glittery flags Mum had made to decorate the hall. We'd sold more than two hundred tickets for the soirée and the buzz around school was so electric you could feel it in your bones.

"Come on!" Alice shouted, leading the way to the hall. "Mrs Eversley said we can spend an hour setting everything up before–" She stopped in her tracks.

"What's wrong?" Archer said.

"Ouch. You trod on my foot!" Liena groaned.

Alice motioned to the other end of the playground

where Mrs Spencer was waving a giant megaphone above her head and some teachers were running around behind her, blocking off parts of the school with yellow tape.

"STUDENTS!" Mrs Spencer announced. "Please wait here."

What on Earth was going on?

"Some pipes have burst in the main building. We believe it's due to the heatwave, so there is no water or electricity in the school hall, canteen or main office block. The classrooms will also be closed until further notice."

"What?" Alice cried, dropping her box of tablecloths on the ground. "But how can we set up for tomorrow? When will the hall reopen?"

"The water board are on their way," Mrs Spencer continued. "But if they say the leak is too extensive for us to remain on school property, your parents will be notified and you will be sent home. And yes, I'm afraid the September Soirée will be cancelled."

"No!" we all shouted in unison.

"This can't be happening!" Archer cried.

"How will we raise money?" Liena said.

"What about the children's home?" Alice bawled.

Don't get me wrong, I've suffered my fair share of disasters in the past. Like that time we tried to take our annual Christmas card photo on the roof and Dad nearly fell off the edge when a helicopter flew over. Or that time Mum bought an animatronic Christmas tree that swayed in time to music and ended up swinging a branch straight through the living room window. But this was a disaster times a trillion. This disaster couldn't be fixed with a quick apology or a new pane of glass. This was a life-changing catastrophe and I needed to come up with a solution pronto.

Miss Eversley gathered everyone from Dickens Class under a giant tree in the corner of the field and asked us to stay there until the people from the water board arrived. We were supposed to be practicing our times tables, but I spent the whole time wondering if I could somehow fix the pipes and save the soirée all on my own. It wouldn't be completely impossible – I'd watched Dad fix the pipes in our old house hundreds of times. Especially that year when he tried to make snow taps and froze the entire heating system. All it would take is a bit of gaffer tape, some pipe cleaners and some Christmas chee— No. No Christmas cheer. I was normal now. I had to do things the *normal* way.

"OK, Lockerton Primary," Mrs Spencer said, striding back into the playground an hour or so later. "I'm afraid it's bad news. The school will be closed for at least a week. Your parents will be called and we must vacate the premises as soon as possible. The soirée, I'm afraid, cannot go ahead."

For a moment, the heatwave dissolved and the world fell dark. I felt like I couldn't breathe. How could this be happening? How could we let Archer and his friends down? And how could I possibly save the day without Christmas cheer?

THE BIG IDEA

32

"What if we held it in the car park?" Alice said, watching Archer pace up and down the playground. "That's no where near the burst pipes and it's plenty big enough to fit everyone."

The thought of a fancy soirée without decorations, music or a dance floor didn't go down too well, especially when Archer pointed out that the water board were running giant pipes and hoses across half of the car park.

"What about *using* the water then?" Liena

suggested instead. "We could make it an underwater theme?"

"I'm pretty sure that goes against all elf and safety ... I mean, *health* and safety rules," I blushed.

There were plenty of other suggestions, like running a bake sale or readathon, but I'm pretty sure ten Christmases will pass before we raise enough money that way! We thought about moving the soirée to later in the year, but that wouldn't give Pa enough time to renovate the house. We even considered holding it on the *roof* of the school, filling the hall with sand bags to soak up the water, or making everyone wear flippers and armbands, but then Archer had an idea that got Alice and Liena so excited, I wondered if Santa Claus himself had flown in to save the day.

"I'm telling you, Holly, it could work!" he said, flailing his arms wildly. "You've got the space and you were going to have a house warming party anyway."

"Yes, but . . . *Christmas themed*? Don't you think it's a bit weird in September?"

"There's nothing weird about it," Alice said, appearing behind Archer with Miss Eversley in tow. "Christmas spreads cheer and we need that now more than ever. Plus, there are already so many fun things to do at yours. Think of the money we could raise."

"I'm not sure," I said, imagining the deafening laughs that would fill the skies once everyone at Lockerton Primary saw our house. "Why can't we . . ."

"Miss Eversley thinks it's a good idea," Liena said. "And so do we. Go on, Holly, say you'll consider holding the soirée at yours."

"I can ask my parents," I said uncertainly. "But do we really need to make it Christmas themed? Don't you think it's sad? Or pathetic? Or strange? What if everyone laughs at us? What if we're run out of Lockerton forever?"

Alice wrapped her arm over my shoulder and squeezed it tight. "Nobody will laugh at you," she said in such a seriously serious tone, I knew she meant every word. "And I'm sorry if we made you feel strange when you joined the school. You were just so confident and cheery and sure of yourself. It was a bit intimidating, to be honest. We didn't know how else to react."

I smiled nervously. So if I was a bit quieter or a bit less cheery, people would've liked me more? If I'd kept my ideas to myself and slipped into the classroom without anyone noticing me, I would've made friends instantly? Brain fog blurred my thoughts as I tried to figure out exactly what they wanted me to do. Was I meant to be loud or quiet? Should I blend in or stand out? Was I supposed to like Christmas or not?

"So . . . you're saying that I should just be me?" I said, wishing I had my Backpack of Cheer to calm my nerves. "And that it's okay to like Christmas? Even if it's all year round?"

"That's exactly what we're saying!" Liena beamed, hugging me from the other side. "Everyone has their

way of spreading cheer, and Christmas is yours. You and your family make people happy. Imagine how much better the world would be if more people spread cheer every day."

I didn't know what to say. I thought school had taught me how to blend in and act normal. I thought I'd finally learnt how to make friends and not be the one that gets laughed at every day. I thought I was growing up or 'finding my feet' or whatever it is you do when you go to school, but now everyone was telling me to act exactly the same as I used to. I couldn't keep up.

"Holly," Archer said, pulling me from my trance. "We can do this. I know we can. But we can't do it without you and we can't do it without Christmas cheer. Please say you'll help us?"

By this point, all of Dickens Class had crowded around us. They were nodding enthusiastically and staring at me like a bunch of eager elves waiting for instructions.

"Okay," I said, feeling a burst of joy erupt from my chest. "Someone pass me a Santa hat. We've got work to do . . ."

THE CHEER IS SPREADING

33

"Lockerton Primary!" Mrs Spencer shouted into her megaphone ten minutes later. "I'd like you all to gather around please. We've got one more announcement before you go home."

We stood at the side of the smelly toilet block, staring out at a sea of faces. Students were huddled in groups for as far as the eye could see. They reached right back to the furthest tip of the field, and parents were milling through the school gates and filling in the gaps. I glanced at Archer, expecting him to be on the brink of passing out like he was during our class rep speech, but his legs weren't shaking, his hands remained outside his pockets and I could tell he was trying hard not to look down.

"I'd like you to welcome some students from Dickens Class," Mrs Spencer continued, motioning for us to stand on the bench beside her. "They've come up with a clever idea so that the September Soirée can still go ahead, so before you go home and start your weekends early, please listen carefully to what they have to say."

Alice confidently brushed the hair off her shoulder and took the megaphone from Mrs Spencer. "Fellow Lockerton Primary students," she said. "We'd like to talk to you about the September soirée and how we've made a few changes. As we can no longer use the school hall, it will now be taking place at Holly Carroll's house, at number twelve Sleigh Ride Avenue."

The crowd broke out into a soft murmur.

"The second change," Liena added, taking a turn on the megaphone, "is that the event will no longer be for Lockerton Primary students only. Invite your parents, your grandparents, your neighbours, your distant cousins, your postie and anyone else you know. We need this event to be bigger than big, because we've got a lot of money to raise."

"In fact, we're going to raise money for the Lockerton Children's Home," Alice said. "Some of you may have heard about the children's home already but –"

"But I know more than all of you," Archer interrupted, grabbing the megaphone from Alice. "Because I live there."

The crowd fell so silent, you could hear a pin drop.

Liena patted Archer on the back and smiled. "Go on, Archie," she whispered, nudging him forward. "You tell them."

Archer cleared his throat. "There's four of us living there at the moment," he said. "Four of us that for one reason or another can't live with our birth parents. It's a place we feel welcome. A place we feel supported. It's a place that feels like home."

My eyes filled with tears, so I found a spot on the

concrete to stare at.

"We don't want you to feel sorry for us," Archer added, his voice getting louder and clearer with every word he spoke. "But we do want your help. Those of us that live there are the lucky ones. I've got some friends that don't even know where they'll be living at Christmas."

He paused to take a breath and scan the crowd.

"We've got the chance to give my friends a home,"

he continued confidently. "A house has come up for sale beside the children's home and if we buy it, we can knock through and make one big house. But we need to act quickly if we've got any chance of buying it and making it liveable in time for Christmas."

A few whispers broke out. Mrs Spencer nodded encouragingly. Miss Eversley removed her glasses and wiped something in the corner of her eye.

"Like Alice said, we were going to use the money

from the September soirée to extend the children's home," Archer explained. "But the burst water pipes have put a stop to that. Luckily, though, my best friend, Holly, has come to the rescue and we think there's a way the Soirée can go ahead." He turned to look at me with sparkling eyes and handed me the megaphone. "Go on, Hols," he grinned. "You're the best at spreading cheer around here."

A rush of energy surged through me as Archer patted me on the back, Alice gave me a thumbs up and Liena handed me a miniature candy cane that she plucked from her pinafore pocket.

"By a show of hands," I said, pulling Mum's crescent moon glasses from my pocket and channelling my best Mrs Claus grandma vibes, "who here knows how to ice-skate?"

Sophie and Dan from Dickens Class put their hands up, along with a few other students.

"Who here would like to *learn* how to ice-skate?" I said.

The rest of the crowd, including Miss Eversley, raised their hands.

"Would anyone like to pet a reindeer?" I went on. "Or help feed a very special donkey?"

Yolandé raised two hands in the air, which prompted the younger students to do the same.

"If you could go sledding this weekend, would you?"

There was a smattering of head nods.

"Would you be brave enough to take on a snow maze? Or enter a gingerbread house competition, toast christmallows over a camp fire, or learn how to make cloudberry jam?"

I watched with glee as their eyes grew wider and wider.

"Would any of your parents like to learn how to make an official apron from Snow Carroll Designs? Would your families enjoy a light show that projects on to our house?"

Marie raised her hand and waved it widly above her head.

"Yes, Marie?" Miss Eversley said.

"Do you live at Disneyland?" she breathed.

Alice shared a look with Liena. "Oh no,' she grinned. "Holly's house is *better* than Disneyland."

The whole crowd burst into chatter, like a flock of robins trying to out-chirp each other.

"As you may have guessed," Alice said, shouting so loud her cheeks turned red. "The September Soirée is no more. This event is going to celebrate spreading cheer and whatever that means to you. Holly and her family will be arranging carols and games and food stalls, and we'll be running hourly craft workshops so you can make your own wreaths and candles and Christmas plates."

"Please bring your own traditions, too!" I yelled over Alice. "The more the merrier."

Alice nodded eagerly. "There will be a small entry fee and costs for each workshop and food stall. And of course, you're welcome to donate more if you want to."

"One hundred percent of the money will be given

to Lockerton Children's Home," Liena added. "There will be news reporters and photographers there, too. So grab a Christmas jumper or Santa hat, and meet us at number twelve Sleigh Road Avenue, from midday tomorrow. It's open to everyone. We really hope you and your families can make it."

Lauren, a usually quiet and nervous student, raised her hand from the front of the crowd.

"Yes?" Miss Eversley said.

"It sounds wonderful," Lauren said timidly. "And I'd, er . . . like to help if I could?" Within seconds, the rest of the Dickens Class shot their hands up, too.

"I can make snowflake paper chains."

"I can ask my choir to sing some carols!"

"I can sell some of my toys to raise more money?"

A lump formed in my throat.

Finally . . .

        the

            cheer

                was spreading.

KEEP SPREADING CHEER

34

The next few hours moved quicker than Santa's reindeer on Christmas Eve, and by the following morning, the heatwave had been replaced by a light rainy spell and a frosty sunrise. If I strained really hard, I could almost feel a chill in the air.

Mum and Dad had done a brilliant job at telling people about the big fundraising event. Dad put banners up around the garden centre, Mum talked about it on the local radio station, and hundreds of students from Lockerton Primary spent their day off school handing posters out at the supermarket.

"OK, Hols," Dad said through my headset. "Is there anything left on the schedule?"

I checked my clipboard and glanced around the garden. "Just the lights and snow," I said, pressing the button on my earpiece so he could hear me. "And the music, obviously."

"You give me the nod and we'll get started," he said.

I did a little jig to calm my nerves. "OK," I said, standing on the pavement so I could see the whole house. "Let's do this. Crank up the Christmasness, Dad."

"Cranking up in three, two, one . . ."

Snow blasted out of the cannons on the roof and fluttered to the ground like tiny puffs of dancing cloud. It covered everything in a glistening layer of white, and instantly made the air feel a few degrees cooler. Next, the lights on the house flickered on, flashing silver and gold, and racing around all four walls, forming different Christmassy patterns. Then the life-size Santa on the roof started shouting, "Ho, ho, ho!" and the speakers hidden under the trees blasted out *We Wish It Could Be Christmas Every Day*.

Bit-by-bit, the rest of the garden came to life. First, the lights around the candy cane archway, then the canopy of lights over the snow maze, the lights that twisted around the humongous fir trees and the light-up signs that directed everyone to the reindeer stables. It was basically a mash-up of Lapland and Las Vegas, except we had way more snow and lights.

"Whoa!" I heard someone shout. "Is this where Santa lives?"

The voice was followed by more gasps and cries of, 'It feels just like Christmas!' And when I turned around, I saw a parade of people walking towards the house, all wearing fluffy red Santa hats and brightly coloured Christmas jumpers.

They flooded into the garden, heading straight for the reindeer rides or photos with Reggie. Some ran headfirst into the snow maze, while others inspected

the hobby trees or signed up for an arts and crafts workshop. Within minutes, the garden was bursting with people spreading cheer, taking photos, laughing, joking and singing along to the festadio.

Mum walked around with trays of mince pies and a bucket for collecting donations. She was wearing a new apron design made with layers and layers of green felt and tinsel, so she was basically a walking, talking Christmas tree. On the end of each layer was a bauble that said *Help Lockerton Children's Home!* and she wore a giant star on her head that said *Thank you for your donation*. Mum sure knew how to make a good impression, and judging by the outfit she whipped up overnight, I still had a lot to learn.

On the other side of the garden, Dad handed out ice skates and showed younger children how to use the push-along penguins so they didn't fall and hurt themselves on the ice. He was wearing his best Father Christmas costume, the one with the shiny buttons and golden thread, and every now and then he'd reach behind a child's ear and pretend to magically pull out a chocolate coin. The children looked at him in wonder, and as he turned back around, he saw me watching him and winked.

I beamed. There he was. The old Dad. The man that made me believe in magic. The man that spreads so much cheer, sometimes I think he could actually *be* Father Christmas.

Over the next half an hour, more and more people swept into the garden, their eyes wide and their smiles wider. I could barely hear the festadio over the squeals and shouts of 'Merry Christmas!' that filled the air, but it wasn't until Archer, Pa and the kids from the children's home turned up that my heart filled with so much joy, it nearly flipped inside out.

"Did you know your neighbours have put their decorations up?" Pa said, pulling me in for a fuzzy red-jumper hug. "They're standing on their doorsteps, handing out mulled wine and mince pies to everyone walking down the street. It's just like Christmas Day!"

I ran into the street to get a better look. Pa was right. Some houses had put fairy lights in their bushes, others had wreaths on their doors and candles in the windows. One had even made a sign that said

Merry Christmas from Sleigh Ride Avenue, and that was when my heart did a jolty-jump, like it had just been super-charged and I suddenly had twice the love to give. Archer and I exchanged glassy-eyed grins. "Excuse me," a tiny voice said. "I made these for you to sell."

I jumped as I felt something pull at my jumper, and when I looked down, a little girl wearing a white fluffy dress presented me with a tray of around two hundred chocolate chip cookies.

"They're a bit squished," she said with a cheeky grin. "I had to hide them under my pillow so Lennie and Rodge wouldn't eat them all. I hope they'll be OK."

"You must be Fran?" I smiled, taking the giant tray from her. "You live with Archer and Pa, right?"

The little girl nodded.

"Well it's jolly good to meet you!" I said. "And I think Archer was right when he said your cookies are the best he's ever tasted. These look delicious."

"He said that?" Fran gasped. "So it *is* him that scoffs half of them before they've cooled down."

Archer looked toward the sky. "I, er . . ."

"Hee-haw! Hee-haw! Heeeeee-haaaaaw!"

"That's my cue," Archer said, grabbing a handful of cookies before Fran could stop him. "I promised Reggie I'd be his personal photographer for the day. Can I borrow the christmacam, Hols?"

"Yes, but don't spoil him too much!" I shouted after him as he shoved an entire cookie into his mouth and ran down the candy cane pathway. "Otherwise he'll never let you leave!"

Laughing, I turned back to Pa. His straw hat was covered in tinsel and stars, and he was carrying a crate of white square cakes that had little brown tags and ribbon attached.

"Now, I don't claim I'm the best at making fruitcake," he said with a grin. "But this is a recipe from my great great grandmother. She used to make fruitcake every Christmas Eve, cut it into tiny squares and then hide it around the house for her children to find on Christmas morning. I thought I could organise a little treasure hunt for the children. Once they find their cake, there's a recipe attached so their parents or guardians can make their own."

"Mr Lenton!" I gasped. "That's brilliant!"

"Please, call me Pa. You're one of the family now, Holly."

He gave me one more hug before following Lennie, Rodge and Fran across the garden, where they were swallowed up by the sea of Santa hats and excited squeals.

"Excuse me," a voice said. "Where are the toilets?"

"Are you in charge? Where should we leave this donation?"

"Is there a bouncy castle? I've heard there's a fairground?"

"Could we get your recipe for that delicious hot chocolate?"

"When do the wreath-making classes start?"

"Hollypops," Mum shouted. "I've got to start the apron-designing workshop now. I'll be in the wrapping room if you need me, OK?"

"Hols?" Dad said, coming up behind me. "Something's happened to the snow cannons. A blockage of some kind. Can you hold down the fort while I climb on to the roof?"

"Sure, I . . ."

I spun around, trying to take everything in. The snow maze was so full, people were clambering over each other just to get out. Kids were having so much fun on the ice, they refused to get off and give someone else a turn. There was no one manning the hot chocolate stall so people were helping themselves and leaving a trail of paper cups strewn across the grass. The snow machines had stopped working completely, and the festadio was somehow playing the same song on repeat, over and over and over again.

Nee-naw nee-naw.

I whirled around. A police car flashed its lights and

pulled onto the grassy verge with its sirens wailing. Then, like a lurking shadow, Mr Bleurgh appeared from a line of fir trees at the side of the garden.Oh no. *Mr Bleurgh!* How could I forget?

"Ahh, officer," he said, approaching a police officer who had angry eyebrows and a deep frown. "You took long enough. These people are hosting a public event without a licence. They're breaking approximately

two hundred and ten committee regulations. Overcrowding is an understatement. And don't get me started on the noise. I *insist* you shut this party down immediately and then remove them from the street."

"Mr Bleurgh!" I shouted over the noise. "We wrote you a letter explaining everything. Didn't you get it? About the children's home and the fundraising and Archer's friends and –"

"I don't open post from strangers," Mr Bleurgh spat. "Especially letters that are decorated with tinsel and stars and . . ." He pulled a face like he was sucking on a sour lemon. "*Confetti*."

"Let's get to the bottom of this, shall we?" the police officer said, placing his hands on his hips. "Who's in charge here?"

I swallowed. "Um," I said, my voice shaking. "I guess that would be me?"

THE CHRISTMAS MIRACLE

35

"I'm PC Padgett," the officer said, looming over me like a storm cloud. "Word reached us about your little event. Do you know you've got hundreds more people on their way? The roads are blocked for miles. People are parked illegally. And there are no signs to show them where to go."

"I –"

"So we've come to see if you need a hand," he said, his face breaking into a smile. "We can close the road off, pop some signs around the village and direct people to the closest car parks."

My mouth dropped open.

"WHAT?" Mr Bleurgh gasped.

"And I'll get some officers to come down and help out with crowd control," added PC Padgett. "It looks like you could use it."

"That would be great," I said, breathing a sigh of relief. "If you're sure you don't mind?"

"Preposterous!" Mr Bleurgh roared. "I called you here to protect the street from these . . . these . . ."

"These kind, generous people doing something for the good of the community?" PC Padgett said, pulling one of our posters out of his pocket.

Mr Bleurgh looked like he might be sick. "But I have a petition!" he yelled, his neck turning that impressive purple colour again. "I have signatures. We don't want them here!"

"That is not a formal petition, Mr Berg," the officer said, looking at the clipboard Mr Bleurgh was waving above his head. "That's just your name written a hundred times."

"But as the Head of the Sleigh Ride Avenue Committee, I . . ."

"Only have the best interests of the residents at heart," P.C. Padgett said. "Yes, Mr Berg, I know. But as the only *real* member of the committee, I'm afraid we can only take this forward as a neighbourly complaint for now. Why don't you try and enjoy the festivities? Everyone else seems to be enjoying themselves."

PC Padgett was right. Neighbours all along the street were handing candy canes to children, hanging more Christmas lights on the front of their houses and joining the growing crowds that entered the snow maze and ice rink.

"So you're not going to help me?" Mr Bleurgh raged, stamping his foot like a child. "You're just going to stand there and do . . . do nothing?"

"I am not going to do nothing," the officer said calmly. "I'm going to help this young lady with her fundraising efforts. Merry Christmas, Mr Berg." And with that, he replaced his cap with a Santa hat and escorted a group of police officers through the crowd, jigging along to the festadio as he went.

Mr Bleurgh glared at me with eyes as sharp and cold as icebergs. I tried to smile and wave a bit of cheer his way, but he hobbled off, muttering under his breath about children's lack of respect and how policing was different in his day. I tried not to let it get to me, but I was pretty sure Who Bleurgh was not the kind of man to give up without a fight, and that thought alone made me more nervous than a badly behaved kid on Christmas Eve. "Holly!" a voice squealed, making me jump. "Sorry we're late. We got stuck in the traffic."

Alice and Liena ran across the road with their parents behind them. They were all wrapped up in bobble hats and velvet jumpers, and Alice had hidden some boiled sweets inside her scarf.

"This is for the children's home," Liena's mum said, handing me a red envelope with a donation inside. "When Liena told us about the amazing things

you do to spread cheer, I thought we were going to see *something* Christmassy, but this is outstanding."

"And we've made dumplings!" Liena said, handing me a long curved plate with a red napkin over the top. "We eat dumplings to celebrate the Winter Solstice, so we thought we'd make some for other people to enjoy."

"Thank you," I beamed, taking the precious plate with two hands. "That's so nice of –"

"Do you mind if I ask you some questions?" asked an enthusiastic man beside Alice. "And maybe take a photo or two?" "That's Elton, my step dad," Alice said. "He's a journalist."

"I think my editor would be quite keen to see an article about this in our next edition," Elton said, pulling a notebook out of his coat pocket. "Would you mind if I . . ."

"Maybe later, El," Alice's mum laughed. "I'm sure Holly has her hands full at the moment."

"Speaking of full," Alice said, her eyes lighting up. "What can we help with?"

"Well, we need to start the reindeer rides soon," I said, reaching into my pocket and handing them some elf helper badges.

"Help with the reindeer?" Liena breathed. "Us? Are you serious?"

"Just make sure there's an orderly queue," I said. "One lap of the garden each. Oh, and collect a pound from each person."

Before they ran off, Alice held her leg out and pointed toward her feet.

"Holly?" she said, her cheeks turning red. "Do you like the elfsolls I made?"

"I *love* them!" I cried, admiring the gold pom-poms on the toes and the tinsel around the ankles. "Maybe we could make them at school? We could start a fashionising club?"

Alice's mouth formed a giant O. "I would love that!"

"Hols?" Dad shouted as Liena grabbed Alice's hand and they ran off towards the stables. "It's bad news, Snowflake. The snow machines aren't working. At all. I could fix them if I could get them off the roof and into my workshop, but I don't think there's time."

"It's fine," I said, wrapping my arms around his soft furry jacket. "Snow doesn't spread cheer, Dad. People do."

I pointed towards the ice rink where Mrs Spencer was helping children on and off the ice. Miss Eversley was cleaning the hot chocolate station and picking used cups off the grass. Even PC Padgett had gathered the police officers around the hobby trees to sing some Christmas carols and a crowd of parents were helping children in and out of the snow maze. I watched Alice and Liena organising the reindeer rides, Pa hiding fruitcake around the garden, and families munching on Liena's dumplings and Fran's chocolate chip cookies. Some families had even brought sweet-filled pinatas from Mexico, and others had brought giant lanterns with spinning lights, which is how they celebrate Christmas in the Philippines.

"Everyone's chipping in," I said. "The cheer is — wait. What is Mr Bleurgh doing?"

CHRISTMAS IS A FEELING

36

Mr Bleurgh was standing in front of the hobby trees, staring into the distance.

"Hyacinth?" he whispered. "Is that really you?"

Mrs Terse, the grumpy lady from the school office, walked out from behind the hobby trees. Her eyes were as wide as an owl's and her bottom lip was trembling.

"Hugh!" she said, blinking hard. "What are you doing here?"

"What am I doing here?" he said. "This is *my* street. What are *you* doing here?"

"I'm supporting the children's home," Mrs Terse said. "Some children from school are fundraising for –"

"So you can come here for some random children, but you can't come here to visit your dear brother?" Mr Bleurgh interrupted.

"You told me not to!" Mrs Terse wailed. "You said I was miserable and you didn't want to be around me."

"You said I was *making* you miserable and that I was sucking the life out of everything," protested Mr Bleurgh.

"*You* said I was being melodramatic and –"

"*You* said I was a sorry excuse of a brother and –"

"*You* said I was the worst sister in the world and you couldn't stand . . ." Mrs Terse suddenly stopped and grinned. *If you could call that a grin...* It was a bit like a cross between Reggie's lopsided smile and Ivy's explosive poo-face.

"What?" Mr Bleurgh said, his grey nose hairs twitching. "What's so funny?"

"I've missed this," Mrs Terse said, reaching out to touch his hand. "I've missed *you.*"

Mr Bleurgh looked so shocked, anyone would have thought he'd seen a flying reindeer.

"Let's face it, Hugh," said Mrs Terse. "We're miserable without each other. Shouldn't we put this little spat to rest?"

Mr Bleurgh stiffened. "I wouldn't call ten years a *spat*, Hyacinth."

"Let's go get a hot chocolate, shall we?" Mrs Terse said, ignoring Mr Bleurgh's temper and linking her arm through his.

Mr Bleurgh let out a deep sigh. "If we must," he said, looking around to check no one was watching. "But only a little one."

"Now *that's* what I call Christmas cheer," Dad said, watching Mr Bleurgh and Mrs Terse trundle towards the hot chocolate stall. "If only we could bottle that feeling."

"You know, Dad," I said, burying myself in his

cinnamon-smelling Santa jacket. "I think Christmas *is* a feeling. It's not a person or a place or a day. It's a *feeling*, and it's that feeling we should try to keep all year round."

Dad squeezed me a little tighter and pulled a candy cane out from behind his ear. "You know what, Snowflake," he said, snapping the candy cane in two and giving me the bigger half. "I think you're absnowlutely right."

THE FRESH START

37

Before we knew it, the sun was setting and the temperature had plummeted. Despite the swelling crowds, everyone had scarves wrapped around their necks and hats pulled over their ears as they huddled together to keep warm. The heatwave felt like such a distant memory, I actually wondered if I'd imagined it.

By seven o'clock, everyone squeezed into the front garden and the street beyond for the light show. Archer and I stood shoulder to shoulder with Alice and Liena just behind us, and Pa and the kids from the children's home to our right. Mum, Dad and Ivy were on the doorstep, ready to flip the switch to start the light show, and it was then that something so unthinkably miraculous happened, I thought I had slipped into a dream.

It was Ivy that spotted it first.

"Know!" she shouted, pointing at the sky in her cute snowflake onesie. "Knooooow!"

A few people looked up.

"She's right!" someone cried.

"No way!" someone else gasped.

"Snow?" Pa breathed like he couldn't quite believe it. "In September?"

I looked up as a fat, fluffy snowflake landed on my cheek.

"Did your dad fix the snow machines, Holly?" Archer said, staring at the snow cannons on the roof.

I shook my head.

"Over there," Alice breathed. She pointed at the grey clouds in the distance. They stretched from one side of the sky to the other, and snow fell from them

like giant clumps of candy floss. "It's real."

Children threw their heads back, trying to catch snowflakes on their tongues. Reggie and the reindeer pranced around in their paddock. Parents scooped toddlers up and sat them on their shoulders. It was like a scene from one of my Christmas card paintings, like someone had reached inside my imagination and cast a spell to bring everything to life.

As the snow fell more heavily, it settled on the treetops and pavements and Pa's shiny red nose. Soon, someone started singing *Let It Snow* and we all joined in, linking arms and swaying from side-to-side.

"Excuse me?" a voice said. "Are you Holly Carroll?"

Two boys were standing behind me. One was quite a bit taller than the other, and he carried a smaller curly-haired boy in his arms.

"Are you trying to make us look bad?" the tall one said, trying to take in the house, the snow and all of the lights. "All I've given Arch is the odd jam sandwich and a go on my skateboard.

Here you are, giving him snow!"

"Eli?" I said, running forward and wrapping my arms around him. "And Carson? And you must be William?"

"My proper name is 'Wreck-It Will'," the little boy informed me. "It's like my secret ifenfity."

Carson laughed. "Yeah, that's us," he said. "You're Holly, right? Archer's new best mate we've heard so much about?"

I nodded bashfully.

"It's pretty overwhelming, you know?" Eli said, his face becoming more serious. "Knowing we won't have to keep moving. Knowing that we get to live with Pa and see Archer every day. It's . . ." He swallowed.

"It's just cheer," I said, my own words getting clogged in my throat. "After all that cheer you've spread to Archer in the past, it's finally coming back to you. That's how spreading cheer works."

Eli grinned. "You're pretty cool, Holly. You and your family. And if there's anything we can do to spread cheer to you, you only have to shout."

I smiled so hard, my cheeks hurt. People really *did* want to help each other. All it took was one good deed that got passed on and on and on and on, and someday soon the whole world would be full of cheer. I could feel it.

"Does Archer know you're here?" I said. "Has he seen you?"

Eli shook his head. "We thought we'd surprise him."

"Archer!" I called, spinning back round. "Look who it is. Have you . . ."

But Archer was staring at the sky. Flakes of snow were caught in his eyelashes and he stood with his hands out, letting it slip between his fingers.

"Real snow," he breathed, trapped in his own little world, his eyes alight like Christmas morning.

"Merry Christmas, Archer," Eli said.

Archer whirled around.

"You've got the snow, Archie," I grinned. 'Now, how about that fresh start?"

THE PRESENT

38

I t took a while for everyone to make their way home. There were a few stragglers taking photos of the hobby trees and a group of parents were asking Mum for present-wrapping advice, but through the thinning crowd, I could just make out Dad and Pa looking at a clipboard, counting on their fingers, and then wrapping their arms around each other.

"We did it!" Archer said. "We actually did it!"

He hugged Eli. Carson punched the air in totitement (total excitement). Wreck-It-Will tore around the garden high-fiving everyone (and everything) he could.

"Pa got the house!" he shouted. "Pa got the house!"

"We're actually going to live with you, Arch?" said Eli. "We don't have to move away?"

"We're going to be here for Christmas?" said Carson.

"Come on, kids!" Dad shouted. "Celebratory hot chocolate and grotto cakes are on me."

Lennie, Rodge and Fran ran into the house, quickly followed by Eli, Carson and Wreck-It-Will, who true to his name, took down two hobby trees and the hot chocolate stall on the way. Pa and Dad walked in after them, patting each other on the back and singing alternate lines to the *Twelve Days of Christmas*.

"We'll be in in a second," Archer called, pulling me back. "Save some for us!"

He dragged me towards the stables where he grabbed a strange brown lump. (No, not reindeer poo, you disgusting people. It was something wrapped in brown paper. But I like where your head was at.)

"I've made you something," he said, handing me the parcel like it was a newborn baby. "It's not very good and the wrapping is terrible but . . ."

"Oh," I teased. "That's meant to be wrapping?"

He cocked his head to one side. "Very funny."

Reggie laughed, too, showing off his long yellow teeth and twinkly eyes.

"It's a good effort," I grinned, turning the parcel over in my hands. "I especially like the holes and crinkles you've added."

"They're, er, not meant to be there."

"I'm kidding!" I laughed, nudging him playfully. "I love that you gave it a go."

"Yeah, well, I hope you like it. I just wanted to say thank you, you know, for . . . yeah."

Reggie nudged Archer out of the way and circled me a few times, sniffing the parcel in case it contained a treat. On top of the lumpy brown wrapping, in thick red pen, were scrawled the words: ALL the things you've taught me.

"It's awful, isn't it?" Archer blushed. "Way too mushy. Just tear the paper. Tear it quickly! Don't worry about reading that bit."

"Stop it!" I laughed, swatting his hands away. "Let me read it."

Archer covered his eyes with his hand.

ALL the things you've taught me. Number one, to be brave and go after the things I want. Number two, to believe in myself and know that anything is possible. Number three, to spread cheer because it will make the world a better place. And number four how to be a good friend.

"You wrote this?" I said. "About me?"

Archer nodded as I peeled the brown paper off as gently as I could. "Archer, this is so unexpec— oh wow."

"I tried to copy what you did, but knitting is harder than it looks," Archer said sheepishly. "I don't know how you do it actually. I thought I just had to wind wool around the sticks but apparently there's a bit more to it than that."

I held a long length of squishy, holey material in front of me. "A scarf?" I croaked. "For me?"

"A friendship scarf," he said. "I know how much they mean to you."

I smiled so hard, my cheeks hurt. "I've never had a present from a friend before," I whispered.

"Well someone once told me that the best kind of cheer was surprise cheer," Archer said. "So I thought I'd give it a go."

I stared at Archer, unsure what to say. My whole body was fizzing with excitetude (excitement and gratitude all mixed up in one), but my jaw was locked shut, like I was really truly properly shocked for the first time in my life. Luckily, being our Expert Awkwardness Detector, Reggie nudged us together for a group hug. He hee-hawed at the reindeer until they joined us, too, and although we ended up having to dodge a few spiky antlers and Reggie's stomping hooves, that moment right there – those few precious seconds – felt even better than Christmas Eve.

Yes, *seriously*.

Do you want to know why?

Because right there, in that moment, I wasn't wishing for anything, or waiting for something magical to happen. I was right in the middle of the magic. With a house on Sleigh Ride Avenue, seven pet reindeer and a diva donkey, a place in Dickens Class with people that understood the importance of spreading cheer, and a best friend for life, *this* is what Christmas was all about. Appreciating what you had. Making the most of every moment. And, of course, spreading –

Parrrrrp.

"Reg-gie!" Archer and I yelled.

"That's worse than one of Pa's!" Archer added.

Reggie chuckled cheekily and swished his tail from side to side.

"This is the best day ever," I said, wrapping Archer's friendship scarf around my head like a bandana.

"It really is," Archer said, scooping a handful of snow off the ground and aiming it right at me. "Merry Christmas, Holly."

THE
END

COMING SOON!

THE
CHRISTMAS
CARROLLS
2

Holly's DICTIONARY

PAGE	HOLLY'S WORD	WHAT SHE MEANS
6, 151	Merrynifiscent	Magnificent
37	Shriekobing	A made-up word
17, 154	Fashionise	A made-up word
31	Hallucitation	Hallucination
31	Sasspicion	Suspicion
35	Despicabelly	Despicably
45	Scorchting	Scorching
49, 128	Sasspiciously	Suspiciously
17, 123	Undubidedly	Undoubtedly
163	Worhusion	A made-up word
167	Silossal	A made-up word
195	Prontocall	Protocol
201	Nercitement	A made-up word
202	Jealger	A made-up word
209	Comspatable	Compatible
251	Contemflate	Contemplate
259	De-poo-sit	Deposit
315	Totitement	A made-up word
320	Excitetude	A made-up word

REAL MEANING

Something really impressive or beautiful

When you don't know whether to shriek or sob

To make high-fashion clothes out of everyday items

When you think you see something that isn't really there

When you think you know something but can't be sure

When someone does something terrible and not at all cheery

When something is hot, hot, hot, hot, hot!

When someone acts strangely and you're not sure why

When you're 100% certain about something

Worry mixed with confusion

When something is SO silly, it's colossally silly

A set of rules or guidelines that everyone should follow

Nervous excitement

When your tummy grumbles and you're not sure if you're jealous or hungry

How well two things work together (e.g. hot chocolate and marshmallows)

Thinking about something for a while

When you give someone a small amount of money to reserve something

Total excitement

Feeling excited and grateful at the same time

ACKNOWLEDGEMENTS
(Also known as Santa's GOOD LIST)

Hi friends!

Holly Carroll (of the Christmas Carrolls) here... Mel tried to write these ack-*noel*-edgements a bazillion times but got too overwhelmed and couldn't find the words to say 'thank you' (which is a bit weird, because I just said it pretty easily!?) so here I am, doing it for her...

As you all know, I love to spread cheer, so grab a hot chocolate, blast out a Christmas Carol and cuddle up under a cosy blanket as I spread some joy and Christmas love to all the people that have helped make Mel's dream come true...

First Mel wants to thank her mum, who has always encouraged her to reach for the stars and follow her dreams. Mel's mum kept her stocked up with pens and notepads when she was growing up, and when Mel said she wanted to study Creative Writing at university and some said 'but what sort of job will that get you?', her mum wholeheartedly supported her and offered to read every story she wrote. Mel's mum definitely has Christmas spirit flowing in her veins, because she's one of the most caring, thoughtful and selfless people on the planet - and she's a pretty good proofreader, too, as it turns out! Thank you, Mel's mum, from the bottom of our hearts!

The next thank you goes to Mel's husband, who witnessed her nearly get published at eighteen and refuse to give up on her dream when she found herself back at square one. He supported her through launching two businesses and running creative writing workshops seven days a week for most of her twenties, and he provided her with endless cheer when running a business, having a baby and publishing a book during a global pandemic got a little intense.

A few more thank you's go to Mel's great grandmother, 'Blue Nan' (for passing down the writing gene), to her best friends (who are the greatest cheerleaders anyone could wish for), to Lauren T (for the advice and wise words when writing this book), to Perdita (who gave Mel the boost she needed to start writing again), to Jo Clarke (for her boundless support and friendship), to authors Abi Elphinstone, Laura Dockrill and Maz Evans (who are some of Mel's biggest inspirations, loveliest friends and favourite writers), and to Russell S (who helped Mel realise she might actually be able to turn her hobby into something more).

Another enormous thank you goes to a very special lady who didn't get the chance to read this story. She always believed Mel would become an author, she loved Christmas almost as much as us Carrolls, and she spread as much cheer as Father Christmas himself. Mel was so grateful for her support and encouragement, and she feels very lucky to have had such wonderful Christmas memories with her Taylor, Aylett and Bessent families.

A last few (but still enormous) thank you's go to the hugely talented Selom Sunu for making us look so magical in the illustrations. To Liz, Olivia, Ryan, Lucy and the whole Farshore team - you really have made Mel's dreams come true and she is so grateful for your time, energy and enthusiasm towards our crazy Christmas story. And to Felicity, Mel's agent - you have been instrumental in telling our story and helping us spread cheer to the world. Mel says you're one of the most inspiring, empowering and joyful people she has ever met, and she feels forever indebted to you for taking her under your wing. You are a true Carroll and expert cheer-spreader, and you are most DEFINITELY on Santa's nice list!

And lastly to you, the reader. Thank you for following along with our story and becoming an honourary Carroll. We hope you sleigh-riously enjoyed it and that you continue to spread cheer with all those around you.

Merry Christmas, one and all, and we hope you've had a Happy New Read.

Love Holly x

MEL TAYLOR-BESSENT

Founder of the hugely successful Authorfy and Little Star Writing, Mel Taylor-Bessent has made her career connecting readers to their favourite authors and encouraging children to write for pleasure. Now Mel is bringing her own writing to readers with her debut fiction series, The Christmas Carrolls.

SELOM SUNU

Selom is a Christian Illustrator and Character Designer who enjoys bringing characters to life visually. Selom has worked on books with KnightsOf and Penguin. He also provides Character Designs for Animation, with Disney TV and CBeebies among his clients.